False Claims at the
Little Stephen
Mine

Crossway Books by
STEPHEN BLY

THE STUART BRANNON WESTERN SERIES
Hard Winter at Broken Arrow Crossing
False Claims at the Little Stephen Mine

THE NATHAN T. RIGGINS WESTERN ADVENTURE SERIES (AGES 9–12)
The Dog Who Would Not Smile

False Claims at the Little Stephen Mine

Stephen Bly

CROSSWAY BOOKS • WHEATON, ILLINOIS
A DIVISION OF GOOD NEWS PUBLISHERS

False Claims at the Little Stephen Mine.

Copyright © 1992 by Stephen Bly.

Published by Crossway Books, a division of
Good News Publishers, 1300 Crescent Street, Wheaton, Illinois 60187.

Cover illustration: Den Schofield

First printing, 1992

Printed in the United States of America

Library of Congress Cataloging-in-Publication Data
Bly, Stephen, 1944-
    False claims at the Little Stephen Mine / Stephen Bly.
        p.   cm. — (The Stuart Brannon western adventure series)
    I. Title. II. Series: Bly, Stephen A., 1944- Stuart Brannon western
adventure series.
PS3552.L39F35 1992   813'.54—dc20   91-43187
ISBN 0-89107-642-5

00		99		98		97		96		95		94		93		92
15	14	13	12	11	10	9	8	7	6	5	4	3	2	1

For a list of other books by
Stephen Bly
or information regarding speaking engagements
write:
Stephen Bly
Winchester, Idaho 83555

For
JUDY and BILL,
partners
on the
trail

ONE

A buzzing sound past his right ear and a simultaneous distant explosion tumbled Stuart Brannon from the back of his horse. Sage strained to bolt, but the rope, looped to a yellow pine log, held hard and fast to the horn.

With .44 drawn, Brannon jerked a '73 Winchester from the scabbard and then fumbled to unhitch his black gelding. At the sound of a second shot, Brannon and Sage dropped to the dirt.

The horse was dead.

Rolling on the ground, Brannon dove behind the log, not chancing a look over the top. A heavy, deep blue autumn sky teased of summer. Masses of white clouds rumbled along like prairie wagons trying to make the pass before the first snows.

Brannon didn't watch. He listened.

And waited. Waited for another shot. Waited for a hoofbeat on the granite rock. Waited to hear dry sticks breaking underfoot. Waited for a shout, or a cry, or a whisper.

"Brannon? What's going on out here?" A squinting Edwin Fletcher shuffled out of the mine entrance and stood shading his eyes with his hand.

Before Brannon had a chance to warn him, two more shots blasted from the rocks somewhere on the other side of the creek. They ripped into the heavy beams at the mine entrance, forcing Fletcher to dive back awkwardly into the dark tunnel entrance.

At that same moment, Brannon rolled and raised up behind the log and fired four quick shots into the distant rocks above which a puff of smoke still trailed. Seeing something like a blue shirt lurch backward, Brannon squeezed off three more rounds.

A yelp and a curse followed by the dust from fleeing horsemen looked to Brannon like a retreat. But he wasn't about to count on it.

"Edwin! Are ya hit?" he called, reloading the Winchester behind the log.

"Good heavens, man, who's shooting at us?" Fletcher, now on hands and knees, stuck his head out of the mine entrance and motioned with his drawn pistol towards the rocks.

"Watch yourself," Brannon shouted as he sprinted for several boulders to the west of the mine. He worked his way forward, one rock at a time. Each time he raised up, Brannon expected to face a barrage of bullets. Fletcher followed, about fifty feet behind.

The water of Trabajacito Creek was lower and colder than Brannon remembered. He reached a small clearing and stooped down to pick up a spent .44-40 center-fire cartridge. The brass shell was still warm. Brannon glanced back at the mine entrance and was surprised at what easy targets they must have made. Then he climbed to the top of the boulders and signaled to Fletcher.

He waited for the Englishman's approach and then followed what tracks he could recognize down the far side of the creek.

"Well, they're gone for now. Looks like there were two of them, but I only heard one gun fire." Brannon squatted and examined some chips of granite.

"Are you going after them?"

Stuart Brannon stood looking down the rolling rocky mountainside. He knew they had already made it to the dark ribbon of cottonwoods lining Trabajacito far below.

"Follow them? Someday. Someday they'll pay!" Brannon pulled his black hat off his head and rubbed the back of his neck. Ten days of stubble bearded his face; anger flashed in his eyes. "I'd follow them to the end of the earth and back this minute—if I had a horse. Everett's got yours, and mine is . . ."

Fletcher looked at Brannon's leather-tough eyes. "Sage?"

"Yeah, the old boy was dead when he hit dirt." Brannon didn't look back at Fletcher. "I rode him up out of Texas, you know. He stood off the Indians at Apache Wells, the cattle plague at Surprise Creek, and that killer of a winter at Broken Arrow Crossing. So now he dies leashed to a log that he couldn't break clear of."

"Well, I . . . " Edwin Fletcher checked his words.

Finally Brannon shouldered his Winchester and turned back to the creek.

"They were after our poke of gold, I suppose," Fletcher offered.

"Nope." Brannon's reply shot out like a bullet.

"I say . . . " Fletcher mumbled. "Well, just what was their intent?"

"To scare us," Brannon replied.

"Scare us?"

"Fletcher, were you scared back there in that tunnel when the bullets started flying?"

"Indeed."

"Well," Brannon drawled, "then they succeeded. I think I may have nicked one of them."

"What do you mean, scare us?" Fletcher pressed.

"Well, from those rocks you would have thought they could hit me sitting up there on horseback. Certainly they had two tries to hit you while you stood there like a Christmas goose." Brannon stooped at the creek and splashed water on his face. It streaked across his beard and poured down the shirt that had once been gray.

"Not everyone shoots straight, Brannon. You disappointed at their marksmanship?"

The men recrossed the creek without speaking and walked slowly back towards camp. Above the lintel hung a hand-scrawled sign: Little Stephen Mine.

Brannon reached Sage and uncinched the saddle. It took both men to pull all the gear out from under the dead animal.

"Do you see where they hit Sage?" Brannon quizzed.

"Behind the ear?"

"Yeah, a perfect shot." Brannon nodded. "They didn't mean to kill us, just chase us off. They killed Sage on purpose. Just to prove their threat was real."

"My word . . . they didn't want our poke; they wanted the whole claim!" Fletcher shouted.

Brannon pulled the bit from Sage's mouth and cut off the remnants of what had been the headstall.

"But why?" Fletcher continued, "No one knows we're up here. No one, including the two of us, knows if this claim is really going to be worth the effort."

"Ah, gold and greed! They do wonders for a man's morality," Brannon commented.

"The prospector has now turned cynic," Fletcher chided.

"Not a prospector," Brannon cautioned. "Just a cattleman looking for a stake. Wasn't it some Englishman who said, 'Gold is a living God, and rules in scorn all earthly things but virtue'?"

"Shelley? You know Shelley?" Fletcher smiled. "You are continually full of surprises."

"Even a drifting cowboy can read," Brannon chided.

"Why, certainly, but Shelley? Out here in Colorado?"

"Is he another relative of yours?"

Fletcher stiffened. "Absolutely not!"

"Well, if I'm right about those old boys trying to scare us off our claim . . . they'll be back." As he talked, Brannon patted Sage's rump as if he were still alive. "What worries me," he added, "is just how they knew we were up here."

"Davis could have mentioned something," Fletcher suggested.

"Everett is one old prospector who knows how to keep a claim well hid," Brannon insisted.

"Oh, I'm sure he can," Fletcher hurried to explain, "but you, yourself, mentioned that he was a good two days late returning from the courthouse at Parrott City after filing the claim and picking up supplies. What if he got waylaid by these ambushers?"

"Yeah . . . well, what if he didn't? If they just wanted to kill, we'd both be dead by now."

"When do you think they'll be back?" Fletcher inquired.

"Maybe two weeks."

"That long?"

"Sure. They'll have to ride over to Parrott or down to Tres

Casas for help and to get that one boy patched up. Then they'll bust in here and toss a few more bullets our way."

"How do you know all of that?"

"'Cause that's what I'd do if I were them." Brannon forced a smile.

"Meanwhile, Davis will be back after filing the papers, and we'll have clear title to the claim," Fletcher insisted.

"Meanwhile," Brannon said surveying the surroundings, "we're going to roll those boulders down here, prop some logs in front, and take turns standing guard."

"But you said they won't be back for two weeks!"

"Yeah, well . . . maybe I'm wrong." Brannon glanced at Fletcher and then slowly plodded towards a shovel.

For eight straight days neither Fletcher nor Brannon worked the claim.

But they did work.

Instead of building a wall, Brannon decided upon a dugout cabin carved out of the mountain itself. Because of the bleak and rocky terrain above their present camp, their white tent offered an easy target. So day after day, the men dug a room back into the mountainside.

Brannon preferred a stout front wall hacked out of big Ponderosa pines, but without a horse to pull them, such a task was impossible. He settled for black pine logs, chinked here and there with globs of thick red clay mud. He didn't peel the bark. He didn't plumb perpendiculars. The roof, at least the narrow part that shot out from the cave, was made of lodgepole beams, brush, and more clay mud. The fireplace was merely a deep fire pit dug back into the cave portion of the room. There was no need for windows. A small front door and four gun slits completed the building.

In front of the cabin they leveled a yard with the tailings from the cave and rolled boulders down to form a low, protecting fence. Finally, they cut a short tunnel from the back of the fireplace. It could hardly be spotted, even from inside the dark cabin.

Most of their gear, except their Long Tom rocker, which sifted out the gold from the silt and stood by necessity next to the Trabajacito, had been moved to the yard or inside. Brannon surveyed their defenses and then carefully marked off the four corners of their claim.

Day by day passed with no sign of another ambush, but Stuart Brannon remained intensely worried. Sitting with his back against the front wall of their cabin, he studied the mountain slope on the opposite side of the creek.

Sage is dead. Everett is missing. And we're holed up like rats. We've got maybe a thousand dollars worth of dust in an old Overland bag. Lord, some things are worth the fight, and some aren't. I sure hope I'm fighting for the right thing!

"You daydreaming of Arizona again?" Fletcher's voice jolted Brannon.

"Prayin'," he responded.

"Same thing." Fletcher shrugged and sat down next to Brannon.

"Not hardly . . . but one of these days, Edwin, you're going to have to ride with me down to my Arizona ranch. It's beautiful, frightful country."

"Not too healthy for cattle, I hear," Fletcher reminded him.

"That's cow country down there. Edwin, I can feel it in my bones."

"What I feel," Fletcher added, "is a chill. Should we build a fire?"

"Must be getting late September. You know, Fletcher, when Everett gets back, we'll have to decide about the winter. The top side of La Plata Mountains looks a lot more rugged than Broken Arrow Crossing."

"I thought we agreed to head south and winter out below," Fletcher declared.

"Yeah, well, that was before some boys decided to help themselves to our claim."

"So you think we'll need to protect our interest?" Fletcher asked.

"No question about it. Maybe we can take shifts up here. I

promised myself no more winters in these mountains. But I don't have enough money to pay the feed bill, let alone buy cattle."

"Those men won't wait until winter, will they?"

Brannon stood to his feet and pointed across to a distant bluff. "If that was a reflection off field glasses that I spotted this afternoon, they won't wait much past morning."

Fletcher bolted towards Brannon. "You saw something?"

"Maybe." Brannon paused. "Just a flash . . . a reflection off some silver . . . or a sun glare from a pair of spectacles."

"Or maybe an old whiskey bottle someone tossed into the mountain?"

"Could be," Brannon agreed. "Anyway, you grab some sleep. I'll ride guard until midnight."

"Brannon, answer me one thing," Fletcher asked, "am I as dirty and grimy as you are?"

"Worse." Brannon laughed. "If I were you, I'd clean up before stopping by to have tea with the Queen."

"Wouldn't that be delightful? A hot bath, clean clothes, a seven-course dinner, and a spot of tea with Her Majesty."

"Well, you get a cave, a cot, beans, salt pork, and a dance with claim jumpers."

"One thing about you, Brannon, you always see the bright side." Fletcher never took his eyes off the distant horizon. "You know, ever since we've met, there's always been some sort of enemy out there. It was the Utes one time. The Rutherford brothers another. Then there's been the weather itself. Now there are some unknown assassins. Do you ever get tired of living on the edge of conflict?"

"Nope."

For a moment only the trickle of the Trabajacito could be heard.

"Nope? That's it? That's all you're going to say on the subject?" Fletcher flung his hands above his head.

Brannon grabbed up his saddle by the horn and dragged it about ten steps to the biggest boulder in front of the cabin. Tossing it down, he plopped down on the dirt and used it for a backrest. "Now, Fletcher, the way I figure it is this. I don't deal

most of the hands in life. So I'm not responsible for whether
they're easy ones or rough ones. But I am accountable for what I
do with what I'm dealt."

"Well, I must admit it's a lifestyle that fits you well. *Tenere
lupum auribus*," Fletcher quoted as he turned for the cabin door.

"But first, we must find the wolf," Brannon added.

Fletcher spun and gave a long, slow stare at Brannon who was
now shoving shells into his breech-loading rifle.

One lone star appeared in the west as the sun finally sank low
enough to let the night break out of the gate. It was Brannon's
favorite time of the day. "Too dark to work and not dark enough
to sleep," he mumbled.

Propped against his saddle, he laid the Winchester across his lap
and stared out between the boulders into the blackening Colorado
sky. *The days come and go, but the nights remain constant.
Camped along the Brazos . . . or the North Platte . . . or in the
Sierras or in the San Juans . . . on a ranch in Arizona or a gold
claim in Colorado . . . the moon, stars, planets shout out with con-
sistency like the faithfulness of their Creator. There have been
other times like these; there will be more like them in the future.*

Brannon threw back his head and gazed at the stars. Then he
closed his eyes and listened. Straining to concentrate, he could
hear a cool breeze in the yellowing cottonwoods near the creek.
A strange distant duet of coyotes echoed up the draw, and an owl
complained bitterly about something.

For the first time in fifteen years he thought of Miss Camilla
Woods. She had ruled the grounds at Pine Springs School.
Educated in Connecticut, she had come to Texas before the war
and had never left, though she made her abolitionist views quite
apparent. Her reward in life was eleven dirty, tangle-haired ranch
children whose only motive for education was to escape doing
chores.

Miss Camilla scolded, threatened, encouraged, and hugged all
eleven for nine straight years. The six boys were madly in love
with her, and Brannon remembered proposing four times himself.

Each nervous encounter was politely refused with, "Stuart, you know I could never marry anyone who isn't proficient in Latin."

Amo, amas, amat.

It was spring when Fatty Barton rode by and mentioned a job pushing cows up the trail for the Double Diamond.

Miss Camilla had walked Brannon to the schoolyard gate. "Remember, Stuart, *'homo doctus in se semper divitias habet.'*"

To which he had replied, "Good-bye, Miss Camilla. When I come back rich, you'll have to marry me."

Somewhere in the brush of west Texas, Brannon knew that little girls were still dreaming of attending New England boarding schools and little boys were still proposing to Miss Camilla.

"*'Homo doctus in se semper divitias habet.'* 'A learned man always has wealth within himself.'" Brannon sighed. "Ah, Miss Camilla . . . but that doesn't make earnest money for a thousand head or even buy a man a cup of soup."

He spent most of the night watching the distant hillside for movement that never came. Fletcher stumbled out of the cabin a little before daylight.

"I say, Brannon, you didn't wake me."

"Well, between nodding off and boredom, I figured one of us needed some rest. Stir up a fire and boil us some coffee. I'll go inside and catch a short nap."

Early morning dreams are often the most vivid and certainly the most remembered. Brannon quickly dozed off and found himself waiting outside a dressmaker's shop for Lisa to try on her wedding gown.

"You've never seen a gown like this one," she teased.

"I hear it's the envy of all the girls in Arizona," he replied.

"Who told you that? Did you talk to Mrs. Weslow?" Lisa grabbed his arm and pulled him across the street. "Let's just say that women for hundreds of miles will be extremely jealous."

"And, I would venture, men throughout the territory are already jealous," Stuart said as he nodded. "When will I get to see it?"

"When I walk down the aisle on my father's arm," she replied with a smile.

The Arizona sun warmed the day early, and Brannon had changed his shirt collar twice before the wedding service began. The church had been crammed with people, most of them friends of Mr. and Mrs. Nash.

After what seemed like hours of waiting, he saw Lisa's father open the big double doors, and then . . .

Voices from outside. Someone laughing? Maybe shouting? That's it, they were shouting.

"Brannon, you'd better get out here!"

"No . . . no, not now . . . not yet." He strained to see the back of the church.

But all he saw was the dark earth wall of the back of the cabin and daylight piercing the gun slits.

"Brannon! We've got company!"

He slung his cartridge belt and pistol over his right shoulder and lifted his Winchester with his left hand. Rather than push through the front door into the bright morning sunlight, Brannon slipped down the tunnel at the back of the fireplace to the mine shaft and then cautiously stepped out to the entrance.

Two men on horseback were talking to Fletcher. One man appeared rather nervous and kept readjusting his bowler. The other one, carrying a rifle, kept glancing at the front door of the cabin.

"Listen again," the red-cheeked man with the bowler said haltingly, "you foreigners are probably unaware of American jurisprudence, but I assure you, this property belongs to Mr. Abner Cheney."

Fletcher held a tin coffee cup in one hand and rested his free hand on the wooden grip of his Colt. By now he had spotted Brannon at the mine entrance. "Are you gentlemen sure you don't want to have some coffee?" He was stalling, waiting for Brannon to make a move.

As the man with the rifle grumbled something about giving Fletcher five minutes to pack his things and move on, Brannon scouted the hillside for others in the group. He hated to move away from the mine entrance without knowing where the others were, and he knew there had to be others. Finally, still half-hidden at the entrance, Brannon decided to make his move.

Completely ignoring the nervous little man, he trained his rifle on the other rider and spoke. "Since you fellas declined Fletcher's generous hospitality, suppose you just move on down the mountain to whatever rat hole you crawled out of."

Both men spun in their saddles; the one with the rifle began to lift it to his shoulder.

"Put it back down, Mister. This ground's too hard to dig graves," Brannon commanded.

The change of focus allowed Fletcher to toss his coffee cup and pull his pistol. He aimed it at the little man, whose horse whinnied, reared up, and crashed into the leg of the man with the rifle, causing that horse to spin a complete circle before its rider regained control.

"We've got all the papers filed at the courthouse," Brannon continued. "You are trespassing on the property of the Little Stephen Mining Company."

"My name is Waldo Vance. This man is Trevor. We're employed by none other than Mr. Abner Cheney himself. As you know—"

"I'll tell you what I know." Brannon stayed half-hidden at the mine entrance as he barked his reply. "I know that Abner Cheney was partly responsible for the Pike's Peak hoax, where many a good man lost his stake and his sanity. I know that a man called Trevor back-shot Judge Payton down at Santa Fe, and he will probably do the same to you before the year's out. I know this claim belongs to Everett Davis, Edwin Fletcher, Stephen Mulroney, and Stuart Brannon. I know you got more men hidden in those hills because you two don't have the fire in your belly to ride in here alone. And I know that no man west of Iowa should get stuck with a name like Waldo Vance."

Vance reached for his bandana and wiped his brow. His horse pranced back away from the little yard.

"Edwin, when I give the signal, shoot old Waldo here in both legs, kick him off his saddle, and take his horse. We could use another animal. He can walk back to—"

"Wait! Wait!" Vance pleaded.

"They're bluffin'," Trevor snarled.

"Wait!" Waldo Vance shouted. "Look, perhaps there is a misunderstanding here. If you'd like to see some papers, I'm sure I could arrange that. We could meet in Parrott or Denver and discuss—"

"I don't want to go to Denver. I don't want to see any phony papers. I don't want to discuss anything. And I don't want to see you on this side of the Trabajacito again! Count to ten, Edwin. Then shoot him," Brannon called.

"One . . . two . . . " Fletcher started.

"You're joking! Man, you can't—"

"Three . . . four . . . "

Vance jerked his horse around and spurred him so hard that the nervous animal shot like a cannonball for the creek. Waldo clutched the horn with both hands and never looked back.

"Five . . . six . . . "

"I don't scare so easy," Trevor growled.

"And I figure there's at least $500 on your head for that job down in Santa Fe. What do you figure?" Brannon didn't flinch.

"Seven . . . eight . . . "

"I'll be back," Trevor threatened as he spun his buckskin and trotted to the creek.

Fletcher and Brannon kept their guns aimed until the two men disappeared over the mountainside. It was Edwin Fletcher who spoke first.

"Brannon, what was the plan if they didn't scare?"

"Shoot 'em."

"You jest, I presume?"

Finally Brannon lowered his rifle and stepped out in his stocking feet towards the yard. "Men like Waldo run every time. There was no chance of him sticking."

"And Trevor? Was what you said about him true?"

"That's what I heard. He's a real *nice* fellow. But he's not stupid. As soon as he can, he'll slide up on his belly like a snake and try to shoot us in the back. His kind always do."

"Listen, Brannon," Fletcher said, reholstering his pistol, "how about letting me know the plan ahead of time?"

"Come on, Edwin, where's your sense of adventure?" Brannon chided.

"Adventure? Adventure! You act like this—" Fletcher turned to face Brannon and froze.

"Howdy, gents," a voice boomed from the hillside above the cabin. "If you fellas so much as cough, you'll get both barrels of this shotgun to clear out your lungs."

Brannon didn't move a muscle, but he could see Fletcher's eyes race across the mountain slope.

"How many are there?" he whispered.

"Four . . . two shotguns," Fletcher answered.

"You figure they'll stay and fight?" Brannon quizzed even as he heard the men moving down the hill.

"Three of them might shoot," Fletcher whispered. "The fourth one is banged up in the right shoulder. I doubt if he could squeeze off that gun."

"You boys are doin' good." The voice was now a little louder. "You jist stay right there till I can collect them guns m'self."

"The one that's bunged up, has he got on a blue shirt?" Brannon pressed. Fletcher nodded.

"Well, good old Waldo and Trevor did the job. They got us in the open so the others could sneak up behind." Brannon turned slowly and faced the four men spread across the mountainside behind the mine entrance and just coming onto the little yard in front of the cabin. One man walked out on the roof of the cabin and sat down holding his shotgun across his lap, dangling his feet over the edge.

A tall, thin man with tobacco stains in his unkempt reddish-brown beard held his double-barreled shotgun to his shoulders and approached Brannon and Fletcher.

"I'm pleased to meet you boys. Joby here told me you done some mighty fine shootin' when you put that slug in his shoulder. Say, you ain't from Missouri, are ya? We got a lot of mighty fine shooters in Missouri."

Brannon ignored the question. "You men know you're trespassing on our mining claim?"

The man on the roof mocked, "Yeah, July, cut out that trespassin', ya hear?"

"Well, they is jist gonna haf to forgive us our trespasses," July responded with a wild grin.

Brannon figured the one on the roof would be no real threat, and the one with a bum shoulder would have to shoot offhand. But he was pretty sure July would let both barrels fly, which, with any degree of accuracy, would separate himself and Fletcher from their legs.

"Coy, jist hep yourself to them carbines and Colts," July ordered.

As the big man wearing a black leather vest stepped up to grab the guns, Brannon motioned with his eyes at Fletcher to dive towards the boulders. When Coy reached for Brannon's gun, Brannon didn't protest, but instead stepped to where Coy would be between him and July. Swiftly Brannon shoved Coy straight back, grabbing the claim jumper's pistol from its holster.

Suddenly there was a shotgun blast, a scream, and a sudden crashing pain in Brannon's back and head. He rolled to the dirt on the downhill side of the boulder fence and struggled to see what was happening. Instantly the blur of a rifle barrel appeared in sight and smashed into his wrist, causing him to drop the pistol.

There were shouts and screams and cries and confusion.

Struggling to his hands and knees, Brannon tried to make sense of his surroundings when he was violently kicked in the ribs and then the kidney.

"Wait!" someone yelled.

There was a blow to the side of his head. The voices started fading as if shouted from a great distance. Brannon felt his head slam into the dirt.

Then he felt nothing at all.

TWO

Acute physical pain has a way of dominating one's attention. Stuart Brannon woke up in the darkness of his own mine tunnel in severe physical pain.

But he did wake up. That very fact surprised him.

For a long time he didn't move. Then he felt a sharp burning throb in the upper right side of his back. His left wrist was stiff and numb. And his head screamed as if someone were beating on it with an axe.

He couldn't remember if there had been an explosion in the mine, or if an avalanche had buried him, or if a stagecoach had run over the top of him. He could feel cold sweat racing off his face. Finally he became aware that he was lying in a puddle of water. His body was fiery hot, but the water was icy cold. With his right hand he struggled to roll himself over on his back. Gasping to regain some steady breathing, he tried to prop himself on his elbow. Then panic hit.

"Lisa!" Brannon shouted, "Lisa, where are you? Lisa!"

A voice, muffled as if from another room, called his name, "Brannon! Listen, man, you've been hurt. Brannon! Brannon, quiet down! Rest a minute."

The voice grew more distinct, and Brannon strained to see who was doing the talking.

"Where's Lisa?" he shouted to the voice.

"My word, Brannon . . . Lisa's gone. Remember? You lost her

in Arizona. Brannon, you've been hurt quite bad. Lie still. If I can get these ropes off, I'll see what I can do for you."

Lisa's gone. Arizona. Colorado! La Plata Mountains. Trabajacito Creek. Gold. Claim jumpers!

"Fletcher?"

"Look, Brannon, you've been pistol-whipped; take it easy," Fletcher consoled.

"Edwin . . . what? . . . Trevor and Waldo Vance, right?"

"They must have slipped in on us while we were sizing up July and his thugs."

Stuart Brannon gritted his teeth against the pain and sat up, still breathing hard. "Did Trevor do this to me?"

"Actually, it was Waldo. Obviously, the restraint of vengeance is not one of his virtues."

"What happened?" Brannon started to remember the scene.

"Well, from my best memory," Fletcher continued, "I dove toward the boulders just as you shoved Coy back. As you can imagine, July panicked and pulled both triggers. The blast killed Coy and the recoil sent July tumbling. I raced toward the creek, but I took a shot in the leg and collapsed just beyond the boulders."

"You got hit?" Brannon gasped. "How bad is it?"

"The bullet passed through without hitting a bone. But it feels like someone sawed off my leg with a rusty, dull hacksaw. But let me go on. I turned to see Trevor bring you down with a rifle barrel against your head. That's when Waldo got brave and started whipping on you with his pistol and his boots."

"Why didn't he kill me?" Brannon questioned. "This isn't much like livin', but it beats dyin', by a little."

"You can thank Trevor for that?"

"Trevor?"

"Yeah, he pulled Waldo off you, and when the little man cocked his pistol at your head, it was Trevor who said, now let me get this right, he said, 'It ain't right to shoot a man who's down and out.'"

"Trevor said that?"

"It does seem rather strange, doesn't it?" Fletcher added.

"Are you tied up?" Brannon asked.

"Just my hands. I suppose they assumed I can't walk on this leg."

"But they didn't rope me down," Brannon stated.

"You looked too near dead to worry about. Besides, where can we go but out the front of the mine?"

"I don't understand why we're alive." Brannon insisted.

"Divine providence perhaps?" Fletcher suggested. "But you and Davis are the theologians. Don't rejoice too much. Before they dragged us in here, Waldo had regained his sanity enough to hatch a plan to hang us."

"Hang us?"

"Quite. I heard him say that Abner Cheney would never be a part of outright murder, so they would try us and hang us for murdering Coy. That way the claim would be vacated nice and legal-like."

"Try us? You mean in a court?" Brannon asked.

"Well, I wouldn't go that far. It seems that Waldo called his henchmen together and proclaimed this mountainside a mining district. He was quickly elected judge. That's when they tossed us in here. I presume they are waiting until you are healthy enough to hang."

"Edwin, can you see in here, or am I blind?" Brannon asked.

"It's dark, but I do know where we are. That new lateral ought to be about five feet behind you. I think Everett's old lantern is there. Any chance you can get to it?"

Brannon pushed himself to his knees. His left wrist wouldn't hold any weight, so he shuffled along on his right arm until he reached the entrance to the lateral tunnel. Finding the lantern against the wall, he struggled to light the wick. Soon a dull glow bounced softly against the mine shaft. He dragged himself back towards Edwin Fletcher.

For a moment, the two men just stared at each other.

"Well, Brannon, I must say you've looked better," Fletcher managed.

Brannon looked Fletcher in the eyes. "Edwin, remind me to retire from prospecting."

"Before or after we're hung?"

Brannon crawled behind Fletcher and untied the ropes on his hands. Then he examined the Englishman's wound. Pulling off his shirt, Brannon began to tie it around Fletcher's leg.

"I say, Stuart, there's no need to use your—"

"Look, Edwin, that shirt is rubbing on my back, so it's more comfortable to pull it off . . . besides, it was getting too dirty for me to wear."

"Well, if you put it so graciously," Fletcher said shrugging. Both men leaned against the dirt wall of the tunnel. "Rather a pitiful situation—two cripples in a cave."

"It will make a terrific chapter in your memoirs," Brannon chided.

"Yes, splendid. Providing, of course, that I live to write them. You will come up with a plan of defense?" Fletcher pressed.

"Defense? I'm afraid our position is indefensible," Brannon replied.

"You mean, there's no hope at all?"

"Nope, I don't mean that. What I mean is we're going to have to take the offense."

"My word, you mean we'll attack them?"

Brannon mimicked Fletcher. "Quite. Can you walk?"

Fletcher shoved himself to his feet and found that by dragging his wounded leg, he could shuffle across the tunnel. "Not exactly with lightning speed," he admitted. "Now just what are our weapons?"

"Surprise and righteousness." Brannon got to his feet. His legs were about the only part of his body that didn't hurt.

"Surprise, I understand," Fletcher commented. "They certainly don't expect us to be mobile. But righteousness?"

"Well, this mine is rightfully ours. They know it, and so do we. A man in the right doesn't need to hold anything in reserve."

"Being in the right doesn't stop bullets in midair," Fletcher reminded him.

"But it does give you a split second to make a decision. I said it's a weapon—it's not a guarantee," Brannon cautioned.

"And if that split second isn't enough?" Fletcher pressed.

"Then . . . " Brannon hesitated. "Then we die doing the right thing. When I meet my Maker, I don't intend on being ashamed of how I got there."

"Now there's a cheery thought for you," Fletcher mumbled. "I say, we really should make some kind of plan. I'm sure they will be coming in here for us soon."

"Then let's set a trap. How many do you think will actually come in here to drag us out?"

"Well, there are five of them left, with one injured. I suppose three might come in, and a couple will cover the tunnel entrance."

"That would be Waldo Vance and Trevor outside, right?"

"I suppose so."

"That would be to our advantage because I don't think July and the other two are long on brains. We'll make some excuse to get them in here, and then we'll jump them and—"

"Wait . . . jump them? You who can't lift your left arm and me who's crippled? Jump them?"

"Look, you'll have your hands behind your back, and they will assume you are still tied up. Then when they go past, you can smash a rock into their lantern."

"And fight it out in the dark without any weapons?" Fletcher gasped. "My word, Stuart, you must have a fever!"

"That beats fighting it out in daylight without any weapons."

"Yes, I see your point, but what about the ones standing at the entrance? How will we get past them?"

"Edwin, you worry too much. I'm not sure we'll even live long enough to be bothered with that."

"Well, that's sincere comfort."

"Look, I'll kill our lantern. You stay here and call out to them. Tell them that I crawled down that lateral and fell into our thirty-foot-deep vertical shaft."

"We don't have a vertical shaft," Fletcher reminded him.

"But they don't know that! I'll bury the first one who comes around the corner with a twenty-pound rock. When his lantern goes dark, roll away from your position. Undoubtedly they will fire in that direction."

"That's it? That's a plan?" Fletcher wondered aloud.

"Well, we can wait to be hung."

"Find your rock and kill the light." Fletcher motioned. "And listen, Brannon, in case this doesn't work out, you'll need to contact the British Consul in San Francisco."

"I have no intentions of it not working out," Brannon snapped.

"No, I don't suppose you do." Fletcher nodded. "Well, we do have one other weapon you didn't mention."

"Oh?"

"Fright. If looking at you doesn't produce Macbethian images, nothing will."

Brannon picked up the lantern and made his way around to the short lateral tunnel. He selected a melon-sized rock, but he could not lift it without help from his useless left hand. Settling for a smaller rock, he clutched it in his right hand and called to Fletcher, "Edwin, are you set?"

"You don't happen to have a better plan, do you, Brannon?"

"No . . . do you?"

"Hardly. Turn off the lantern."

Within seconds, Fletcher let loose a chilling scream.

"Vance! Vance! Get in here! Hurry! Brannon's fallen down the shaft! Hurry!"

Noises and shouts filtered back from the mine entrance, and then a flicker of light slowly made its way toward Fletcher and Brannon.

The Englishman kept up the yelling. "My word, hurry. He must have crawled down that lateral tunnel and fallen down the shaft. It's thirty feet deep! Hurry, I can hear him groaning! Hurry, you blokes!"

Peering through the dim light, Brannon could barely make out July and one other man. But instead of brushing past Fletcher, they cautiously leaned into the tunnel and fixed their guns on Edwin.

"Where's the other one?" July demanded, not taking another step but holding the light above his head.

"Good heavens, man! Haven't you heard what I said? Hurry, I think he crawled back to that side tunnel and fell down a shaft. Right over there!" He motioned with his head.

"Right convenient of him." July spat a wad of tobacco against the far wall. "How'd ya git that shirt wrapped around your leg?"

Brannon put his bum left hand to his mouth and muffled a deep groan.

"Don't just stand there. I mean, at least they shoot wounded horses to put them out of their misery," Fletcher insisted.

"He's right, July," the other man said. "They shoot horses. Can I shoot him, July?"

"Trevor and Waldo won't like it," July cautioned.

"Them two is crazy. He is a mumblin' and groanin'."

"Ahh!" Brannon moaned, cupping his hands around his mouth and projecting his voice toward the far end of the tunnel. "*Hoc age!*"

July pointed his pistol in the direction of Brannon's voice. "What did he say?"

"He must be out of his mind," the other man responded. "He said something about hawks? Hawk ah-geh, or something like that? Kin I fire a few shots down the tunnel, July?"

Suddenly, Fletcher sat up. *Hoc age?* Instantly, he threw a rock into July's raised lantern. The kerosene sloshed down the claim jumper's leg and ran into his boot.

Dropping his gun, July flung the lantern aside as it burst into flame, igniting his pants and dripping flames into his boots. In panic he screamed and ran towards the tunnel entrance.

His partner fired at the dark end of the tunnel in the direction of Brannon's voice. But realizing that July carried the only light in his boot, he turned to retreat and ran headlong into a round of bullets that those at the tunnel entrance were pumping into the mine once the burning July had made his hasty exit.

"Edwin, are you all right?"

"I presume that is a rhetorical question."

"Well, stay down. They'll probably pump some more lead back our way."

Another dozen shots rang down the tunnel; several ricocheted close to Brannon. Slowly, he inched his way in the dark closer to the downed man. Finally, still keeping close to the ground, he pulled the gun out of the man's lifeless hand and unfastened the cartridge belt. Searching the man's boots, he found what he expected—an Arkansas hunting knife.

"Edwin," Brannon whispered. "Where are you?"

"Somewhere between extinction and absolute terror! Over here!"

Six more shots whistled down the tunnel and crashed into the pilings behind the men.

Lying on his back, Brannon loaded the chambers of the pistol in the dark and handed the knife, handle-first, to Fletcher. "Take this knife and follow me."

"Follow?" Fletcher gasped. "We're actually going out?"

"Yeah, I'll fire some shots, and they'll back away from the entrance."

"You suppose we could make it to the tunnel that leads into the cabin?" Fletcher asked.

Several more shots came ringing down the mine.

"Maybe . . . and maybe they haven't discovered the connection. And maybe no one will be in the cabin, and maybe they will all lay down their guns and give up."

"I say, Brannon, are you sure you're quite well? That was several nasty blows to the head," Fletcher quipped.

"Nasty blows? Is that what you call it? Edwin, you have a gift for understatement."

"Yes, well really, Brannon, are you sure this is best? Perhaps we should take time and consider alternatives. Can't you think of one that allows us to survive?"

Ignoring his question, Brannon instructed, "Keep right on the ground behind me. Don't raise up for anything, and stay to the far wall of the tunnel. I'll stay on this side, and maybe one of us will make it."

He fired three shots at the entrance, now appearing as a faint light in the distance. Then he and Fletcher crawled down the tunnel. Brannon reloaded and fired two more shots. Spotting the entrance to the side tunnel through the light filtering in from the entrance, he rolled to the far side of the mine wall next to Fletcher.

"Now! Get in there!" He shoved Fletcher into the short side tunnel that led to the cabin.

Joby, the claim jumper with the shoulder wound, suddenly leaped to the cave entrance and awkwardly raised his rifle, but Brannon's bullet caught him in the chest and slammed him violently backwards. Stumbling down the tunnel over the crawling Fletcher, Brannon took one quick glance inside the cabin, and then staggered out into what he perceived to be an empty room.

He was wrong.

Waldo Vance had spent most of his life behind ledger sheets counting other men's fortunes. He wore cheap suits and factory shoes, and he lived in rundown boardinghouses that always seemed to look up at a fancy place on the hill. He was driven with the prospect of living in that big house himself. *He* would ride about in the gold-trimmed carriage. Beautiful women would clamor just to sit in his box at the opera. It was a wistful dream that sustained him through countless boring seasons.

Now, as a trusted employee of Mr. Abner Cheney, Waldo had his chance. Cheney had more or less promised to take him in as a partner if he could legally secure deed to the Little Stephen Mine. It was that promise that drove Waldo out into the mountains of southwest Colorado, pushed him into a dirty, sweaty land, and forced him to crouch against the wall and point a loaded pistol at the squatty black tunnel entrance that looked much like a fireplace hearth.

Stuart Brannon burst into the cabin and stood up, stretching out his cramped back. On impulse he whipped around to check out the one wall he couldn't see before entering, and he came face to face with a raised pistol. Waldo Vance had never shot a man point blank before. He froze for a split second.

At that moment, Edwin Fletcher limped through the tunnel screaming, "Waldo!" and slashed at the little man's arm with the gigantic hunting knife.

With blood seeping through his ripped coat and shirt, Waldo dropped his weapon and fled for the front door.

Brannon scooped up that gun and followed him out the door with one weapon in his right hand and the other tucked into his belt. He expected he would see just how good Trevor was with a gun, but with the burst of sunlight there was only silence.

Brannon squatted down behind the boulders in the front yard and tried to take stock. One gunman lay on his back near the mine entrance. It took only a glance for Brannon to know that he was dead. Waldo Vance pathetically circled his frightened horse trying to grab the reins with his left hand while clutching his jacket around his wounded right arm. Suddenly a scream vibrated from the region of the Trabajacito. Brannon, with Fletcher limping at his side, proceeded towards the creek and Waldo Vance. Fletcher had picked up July's shotgun from the yard, but he didn't know if it was loaded.

Seeing the men approach, Vance literally threw himself on the horse, half-riding, half-sprawled across the saddle. Making it to the cottonwoods on the far side of the creek, he cut behind them and dropped out of sight.

Brannon and Fletcher looked toward the creek and saw July lying in the cold, shallow stream.

"Where's Trevor?" Fletcher demanded.

"He's done left me here to die! That's what he did! My leg's done burnt off, and he just rides away sayin' he don't do business with amateurs. Well, I'll show him who's who!"

If it hadn't have been for the deadly seriousness of the moment, the scene would have been humorous. With scorched leg cooling in the water, an unarmed man hurled curses at a professional gunman.

"Well, July, it's nice to see someone enjoying the water."

Still seeing no other movement, Brannon signaled for Fletcher to join him.

"Edwin, keep him covered while I round up his horse. If he moves, shoot him in the head with that shotgun. No use unnecessarily wounding a man."

July looked in panic towards Fletcher.

"The man's all heart." Fletcher smiled and pointed the shotgun at July's head.

The man in the creek didn't move.

As he suspected, Brannon found four horses picketed by the

rock on the far side of the Trabajacito, near the site the gunmen had used the first time they had shot into the mining camp.

Returning with all four horses in tow, Brannon ordered July out of the creek.

"On your horse right now!" he raged.

"I'm a dying man," July complained. "If I get out of this water, the pain in my burnt leg will kill me."

"If you stay there, Fletcher will turn you into fish bait."

"It ain't fair!" July shouted.

"Fair!" Brannon shouted. "Fair?"

At the anger in Brannon's voice, July flung himself out of the water and, dripping wet, lunged for his horse.

"Fair?" Brannon continued, "Edwin was leg-shot, and you tried to pistol-whip my head like a snare drum!"

"Ain't me. I never touched ya. It was that Waldo. He went plumb insane. I told them they ought to jist shoot ya."

Brannon let July struggle to mount his horse.

"Ya cain't keep them other horses. They belong to the boys," July insisted.

"You can tell their next of kin to come up and make claim to their belongings," Brannon replied. "All they got to do is pay the feed bill and bring burying money." He slapped July's horse, propelling the rider down the trail and into the woods.

Fletcher and Brannon waited for him to disappear from sight.

"Will they bring more men next time?" Fletcher asked.

"If they do, it would be good news." Brannon gingerly bent down to the creek and began to splash cold water on his shirtless back and his red, raw face.

"Good news? I don't follow."

"If somebody wants this mine that badly, then it's a cinch that we struck it rich. That last poke Everett took in must have sampled out real pure."

"Which means that Davis must have made it to the courthouse at Parrott City!" Fletcher sat down next to the water's edge and unwrapped the bloodied shirt from his throbbing leg. He soaked the cloth in cold water, wrung it out, and then retied it around his leg.

"Yeah, he must have made it to town, but he hasn't made it back."

For two days Brannon and Fletcher did little more than tend wounds, eat, and rest.

Stuart Brannon slept very little.

Not having a wearable shirt left, Brannon spent the heat of the day shirtless and the rest of the time in his tattered jacket. His head, still badly bruised, could not carry the weight of his hat.

Brannon sat out at the campfire as daylight faded, scraping the beans from a tin plate with his knife.

"We need to get you to a doctor," he suggested.

"Me?" Fletcher questioned.

"Your leg wound is still way too puffy. That bullet went clean through, but maybe it shattered a bone or something."

"Me? My word, Brannon, you haven't slept in days, and when you doze you wake up screaming about Lisa. You're the one that needs help," Fletcher insisted.

"Look, if my skull's cracked, it's cracked. There's nothing any doc can do with that. If my screaming keeps you awake, I'll go out and sleep in the woods."

"It's not that, Stuart, and you know it. It's just . . . well, listen, Col. Henderson once took a bruising blow from a rock slide in the Punjab. He marched us around the mountains for two weeks claiming everything was fine, and then he dropped over dead, just like that."

"Thanks for the encouragement. But the truth of the matter is, there was nothing you could do about it anyway, correct?"

"Oh, I suppose not, but still—"

"Listen, in the midst of that beating the other day, something happened to me that has never happened before." Brannon tossed down his plate and lay back on the dirt. His back cramped, and he immediately sat straight up. Rubbing his shoulder, he continued, "You see, ever since Lisa and the baby died in my arms down in Arizona, I swore that I would never let her loose. I mean she might be buried in the ground and her sweet soul gone to heaven, but I have never for one second of my life released her from the center of my heart and thoughts."

Brannon stood and turned around with his back toward Fletcher and the fire.

"Well, the other day in the midst of that beating, I felt my self-control slipping away. And, just for a moment, Edwin, I found that I didn't care about helping you, I didn't care about Everett, I didn't care about Elizabeth and Littlefoot, I didn't care about an Arizona ranch scattered with dead cows, I didn't care about a still-born baby, and . . . " He took a deep breath, but there was absolutely no way he could say it.

Fletcher filled in the sentence, "And you didn't care about Lisa?"

"It was the vilest, blackest, most depressing feeling I've ever experienced. Death would be a reward compared with that. I suppose that's why I'm afraid to doze off. I'm scared that the feeling will come back."

"I grieve for you," Fletcher said softly. "And I grieve that I never had the opportunity to meet her. She must have been quite a woman to captivate you for so long. I wonder, though, if she would approve of your actions now?"

"Most certainly she wouldn't." Brannon turned back to the fire. "She would be insisting that I put her in the past and get on with my life . . . and she would also know that there is no human way possible for me to do that."

"Like a scar you carry for life?" Fletcher offered.

Brannon spun toward Fletcher. "You're going to town tomorrow."

"What?"

"Take the horses for supplies, check out every boardinghouse run by widows and every cafe that sells apple pie. Everett has got to be somewhere. Don't come back without him and the deed."

"And a couple of shirts for you?"

"Ah . . . yeah."

"Perhaps we should both go," Fletcher suggested.

"I'm not leaving this claim until we go broke or make enough money to buy cattle for my ranch."

"What if I refuse to go without you?" Fletcher questioned.

"Then I'll hogtie you and strap you to one of those ponies."

"I'll go," Fletcher finally offered.

"Leave about sun-up, and you could get there in four or five days."

"You won't do something rash while I'm gone, will you?" Fletcher asked.

"Rash?"

"Like collect all our dust and head for the Mexican border!" Fletcher said laughing.

"No chance." Brannon smiled for the first time in days.

"No, I suppose you're right," Fletcher added, "no chance of that at all."

THREE

The two men finally agreed that Edwin Fletcher should go to Parrott City and even Tres Casas, if need be, to find Everett Davis and bring back supplies. Brannon insisted that he take all three horses.

"But you'll need some mobility," Fletcher cautioned.

"The chances of there being any horses to buy in Tres Casas is remote. With gold fever running high, horseflesh will be at a premium. And there's no way to make it through another Colorado winter without two big packs of supplies. Ride the sorrel and load the other two."

"You're sure you'll be safe?" Fletcher asked as he mounted the brownish-yellow gelding.

"Safe? Me?" Brannon started to laugh, but then checked himself as a sharp pain shot through his upper back. "Look, I've got food, water, enough bullets for Sherman's army, thanks to those old boys' saddle bags, and a gold mine to dig. What else could a man want?"

"Well, I'll be back in ten days to two weeks, with or without Davis, supplies, and filing papers. You can count on it," Fletcher promised.

"Edwin, if you're not back in two weeks, I'll figure you're dead. I'll probably ride into Denver and celebrate."

"Not likely. If I'm dead, you'll spend the rest of your life tracking down the bushwhackers." Edwin turned his horse and led the other two across the Trabajacito.

Brannon watched him until he plodded behind the cottonwoods.

Yeah, that's me. Predictable as mud.

For the first time in ten months Stuart Brannon found himself
alone. It was a bittersweet feeling.

He began to organize camp for a one-man defense. Thanks to
the three fallen gunmen, he now had two rifles, three pistols, and
a double-barreled shotgun. Brannon stashed the shotgun and
shells across one of the ceiling beams in the cabin. He buried a pistol at the deepest part of the mine so he would never be trapped
inside defenseless again. One rifle and a box of shells was just
inside the mine entrance in the short entry leading to the cabin.
Another pistol rested in his gun belt, and the third bounced in the
back of his jacket where the torn lining had created a pocket. He
toted his Winchester everywhere.

Brannon felt confident he would have an even chance in any
direct confrontation. Most riders would have to come right up
Trabajacito Creek and then across the water and out of the trees
into the opening. The mountain slope above and behind the mine
entrance bothered him. It was a rocky hillside devoid of trees.

His only solution was to randomly set the four big double
underspring traps (that Everett Davis had insisted they bring
along) amidst the brush and boulders on the mountain. Then he
rolled the rocks around to funnel foot traffic right over the tops
of the concealed traps.

Brannon figured the traps had only a remote chance of holding
off an ambush, but at least they gave him a little hope.

"There's no good reason for anyone to come down that slope,"
he mumbled.

For Stuart Brannon, the prospector's life was a dull, boring
grind. And now, finding himself all alone, it was almost mindless.

His left hand only ached when he lifted something heavy.

His back only cramped up when he lay down.

His face . . . Brannon didn't bother looking at his face.

Dig a cart load out of the darkness of the mine.

Wheel it down and pour it in the long Tom at the river.

Sift it out.

Pick out any color that turned up.

Go back for another load.

The way Brannon figured it, the mine was just good enough to pay expenses and give each of them a little profit.

One day for a calf. Two days for a steer. Three days for a cow. That's what kept him going. When he reached five hundred head, he would sell his share to the others and go back to the Arizona ranch.

Eight days after Fletcher left, Stuart Brannon splashed water on his face and realized that his back didn't hurt. His left wrist was functioning, although it couldn't yet keep up with the right one. His beard was about an inch long, and it concealed the bruises that were healing and turning yellow on his face. His hat was back on his head, and his steel gray eyes once again clear. The throbbing headache that had dominated every waking moment disappeared completely.

Something about the feel of the morning made Brannon expectant. He thought maybe it was the thin film of ice on the water left in the wash basin that reminded him the season was changing fast. The bacon tasted saltier, and sourdough bread from the Dutch oven was fresher, and the coffee lifted him right up onto his feet. Maybe it was the warmth of a breakfast fire. Or just maybe because it was the first night in weeks that he slept without a nightmare about Lisa.

This is a good one! This is just the kind of day to have old Everett and Fletcher come riding down the trail! It wouldn't surprise me if a plump turkey waddled into camp, pulled all its feathers off, and jumped into the pot. Bring them back safe, Lord . . . bring them back safe.

Looking at his bean pot, he reached over and dumped in four times the normal supply to soak. "If I have company," he mumbled, "they'll be very, very hungry."

The sun was straight above and fairly warm, but Brannon worked in the dim glow of a lantern at the deepest part of the mine. Shirtless, he felt the sweat roll off his strong shoulders leaving tracks in the dirt that clung to him. It was pointless to wear a wide-brimmed hat while swinging a pickaxe, but Brannon insisted on it. He was a cattleman, not a miner.

He exchanged his pick for a sledge and drill when he came to a rocky outcropping deep in the tunnel. He knew it was time for a nooner, but he wanted to chip off one rock ledge before he stopped to eat. Squinting his eyes almost shut to keep the rock chips from spraying him, he pounded away. The echo of cold hard steel hitting cold hard steel numbed his ears. He could feel his shoulder muscles start to burn and ache, but there was no sign of the rock giving way.

"Just three more swings . . . just three more swings!" he kept telling himself. When at last the ledge broke off, Brannon dropped to his knees just to catch his breath. For a few moments he stooped there on hands and knees panting and staring at the dark tunnel floor.

He didn't bother looking at the sample rock. It was too dark in the tunnel to tell much of anything. Heaving a deep sigh, he rose to his feet, grabbed the sample with both hands, and trudged out to the little yard in front of the cabin where the breakfast fire was only a faint wisp of smoke. He dropped the rock like an anchor beside the fire.

Brannon stirred up the coals, added a few sticks, and scooted the bean pot a little closer. He smiled as he saw the huge batch of beans. "For supper," he mumbled, "I guess they're coming in for supper."

Starting for the creek with the empty wash basin, he suddenly remembered the rock sample. Turning back to the fire, he hefted the boot-sized piece and turned it over, holding it in the direct sunlight.

Brannon gazed in awe for several minutes. Finally his mind caught up with his eyes. A definite deep yellow vein of metal coursed through the rock. Any direction he turned the rock, the metal reflected the same gold tones. Taking his knife, he pried away a thumbnail-size leaf of the metal and mashed it together with his fingers. Finally, he pulled his gun from the holster and, using the butt end, hammered the metal flat on a rock.

"Constant color . . . malleable . . . veined in bedrock!"

Brannon tossed down the sample and ran back to the mine tunnel. Barely stopping to relight the lantern, he dashed to the spot where the outcropping began. Running right back into the rock was an increasingly wider vein of the yellow metal.

"The lode! Davis! Fletcher! Little Stephen! We did it! We found the lode!"

Running out of the mine tunnel, Brannon forgot his ever-present Winchester. He grabbed the ore sample and began to shout and dance around the fire.

"Brannon, you lucky dog! I knew it was going to happen today! I knew it! Six hundred head of fine Mexican cows. No! Six thousand head! I'll have to buy another ranch!"

Instantly, Brannon froze in the midst of his dance. There, not three feet from the boulders at the edge of the yard, stood three Indians.

Two were in buckskins, and the third wore old canvas duckings and a red wool shirt. Since all three held rifles, Brannon hesitated to go for his pistol.

"You got food?" the one in the red shirt asked.

"You speak English?" Brannon questioned.

"Do you speak Ute, Navajo, or Shoshone?"

"No, but I do know some Apache," Brannon offered.

One of the buckskin-clad braves spat on the ground. "Dogs!" he growled.

The red-shirted Indian smiled. "Little Eagle's wife ran off with an Apache."

"Dogs!" the other Indian repeated.

"You got food?" The third Indian who had remained silent pointed to the bean pot.

"Well," Brannon said relaxing his tense muscles, "come on. I was expecting you, sort of."

All three Indians piled plates high with beans and tore off huge chunks of bread.

Brannon sat cross-legged on the other side of the fire from them watching their every move. He wished he had his Winchester beside him, as they did. He ate his dinner with one hand close to his pistol grip. After several minutes, Red Shirt looked up.

"You knew we come?"

Brannon started to explain that he was expecting others, but as he tried to figure out how to explain it, the Indian continued, "I told them you would know we were in the trees. We have watched your fire for days, and you have watched ours. You are the Brannon, no?"

"You know me?"

"Are you the Brannon?"

"I'm Stuart Brannon." He let his hand slip a little closer to his pistol. That move did not go unnoticed by the Indians.

"Spotted Horse, his sister, and papoose ride north with us when the grass was green."

"Elizabeth? You know Elizabeth and Littlefoot?"

"Yes, and we know the Brannon." He smiled.

"What did she say?"

"She said you took her into your tent and treated her well when she was very wounded. She said that you have a God that makes you do what is right even if it costs you your life. She said that you are a brave warrior and a good man."

"Did she get back up to Oregon? To Chief Joseph and the tribe?"

"I do not know," he answered, "but I hope not."

"Why?"

"The Nez Perce—they are fighting the soldiers."

"A war?" Brannon pressed, "In Oregon?"

"No. In Idaho or Montana, I have heard."

"But her family is in Oregon."

"It is Joseph who leads the battle."

One of the other men spoke briefly in Ute and then pointed towards the mountain behind the mine entrance.

Red Shirt acted as interpreter. "He asks why you trap beaver where there is no stream and bear without bait."

Brannon looked back at the mountain. "The traps? You can see the traps?"

"We watched you bury in the ground."

"You've been out there that long? Why did you come in now?"

Red Shirt smiled, revealing dimples at the corners of his mouth. "We were hungry. Hunting is not good."

"The traps are for bad men."

"Bad men? Are you expecting a battle?"

"Perhaps."

"Why do they want to kill you?"

"Well . . . " Brannon hesitated. "I'm digging for gold, and they want to take it away from me."

"The mountains are full of gold men. It is foolish. Look at you, your clothes are torn, you have no shirt, your boots are worn thin, you are dirtier than ten warriors. You spend the whole day in a hole in the ground like a squirrel. Why would anyone look for gold?"

Brannon just stared at Red Shirt.

Then one of the others spoke, and Red Shirt interpreted. "You got bullets? We trade for new bullets."

"Maybe I have new bullets, but I will need them for the bad men. Besides, how do I know that you won't shoot me with them?"

Red Shirt once again revealed his dimples. "How do you know we won't shoot you with these old bullets?"

Brannon stood to his feet slowly. "If I trade you new bullets, what do I get?"

After a moment of consultation, Red Shirt offered, "A shirt."

"You don't get many bullets for a shirt."

"And," Red Shirt continued, "we will give you news."

"News?"

"Yes, we will let you know when the bad men come so you might be ready to fight."

Brannon pushed his hat back. "But when the bad men arrive and shooting begins, which way will your guns be pointed?"

"When the shooting starts, we will be gone," Red Shirt admitted. "We will not fight your battle."

"That's fair." Brannon continued, "Two boxes of bullets. One for the shirt and one for the news."

"Three boxes," Red Shirt insisted. "It is a very fine shirt."

Having completed the bartering, the three Indians recrossed the Trabajacito and meandered downstream.

Brannon admired the soft, bleached white deerskin pullover shirt. "It is, indeed, a very fine shirt," he noted to himself. "A little worn, but very fine." He retrieved a basin of water and scrubbed himself from the waist up. Then he rooted around in his war bag for a straight razor. Using the blade of the big Arkansas knife for a mirror, Brannon shaved off his beard, leaving a rather full mustache. He pulled the shirt on and tucked it into his trousers. Then he combed his hair for the first time in a week. He placed his hat on the back of his head and grinned.

When he tossed the razor back into the bag, he got a glimpse of the gold locket. He pulled it out and looked down at the smiling photograph of Lisa Nash Brannon.

"Well, Darlin', how do I look? You know, for an old cowhand turned rich prospector?"

Brannon glanced at the knife mirror once more.

"You're right. It's got to go. You never did like a mustache, did you?"

Within moments, his upper lip was clean shaven.

Brannon spent the rest of the day chipping away at the gold vein to determine its size and direction.

"Everett, where are you when I need you?" he mumbled. "This thing spreads wider and sinks into the ground! If this keeps up, we'll have to blast a vertical shaft, get pulleys and cables and a donkey engine—no doubt pump water; it's already almost too wet to work . . . "

"What am I doing?" Brannon muttered as he walked out to the mine entrance. "I used to be a respectable cattleman, and now I wander around in the guts of the earth talking to myself about a subject I know nothing about!"

As he broke into the clearing in front of the mine entrance, he realized that he was once again covered with the grime of the diggings. Red Shirt was stirring his fire.

The Indian turned and nodded. "The Brannon let the beans get cold."

"Help yourself," Brannon offered, but Red Shirt had already dipped out a coffee cup full of beans.

He finally paused long enough to talk. "You will have visitors."

"Bad men?"

"Weak men. They will not fight."

"How many?"

"Two. One young. One not so young," Red Shirt reported. "They pull a black wagon."

"A team and wagon? Up here? Maybe it's Fletcher and Davis with supplies!"

"These good men?"

"Yes, they are my partners."

"They dig in the hole too?" Red Shirt questioned.

"Yes, yes, this mine belongs to us." Brannon impatiently paced, looking down to Trabajacito to catch a glimpse of the wagon.

"No," Red Shirt added, "only the hole belongs to you. The earth and metal belong to the Creator. These men are not your partners. They have never dug in dirt."

"What do you mean?"

"They are too clean. Besides, one is very young—only a boy."

Red Shirt took another mouthful of beans and then walked back down to the creek and disappeared behind the trees.

The screech of under-greased wagon wheels preceded the appearance of a black canvas-covered wagon pulled by two teams of mules. Driving the team across the Trabajacito was a gray-bearded man wearing a flat metal helmet that almost looked to Brannon like an upside-down pot.

Brannon stood halfway between the mine entrance and the creekbed, watching as the wagon rumbled his way and came to an abrupt halt. The driver tipped his hat to Brannon and barked orders to the boy sitting beside him.

"Gilmore! Don't just sit there! Unhook the mules and water them!" Then, climbing off the wagon with some effort, he turned to Brannon.

"Good day, sir. Sorry for this intrusion. I have no intention of imposing on you."

"Are you a peddler?" asked Brannon, still shirtless and dirty from digging in the mine. His Winchester '73, gripped in his right hand, lay across his shoulder.

"Sir! I am a professional man—Hawthorne H. Miller, photographer. Perhaps you've seen some of my works?"

"Well, not out here I haven't." Brannon smiled. "You fellows want a little chuck? Just help yourselves."

"Chuck?" Miller tipped his head to one side.

"Food, Mr. Miller," Gilmore chimed in from in front of the mules.

"Oh, yes, certainly, why thank you, sir," Miller fussed. "It's a pleasure to find such hospitality way out here in the middle of . . . by the way, where is this?"

"Colorado." Brannon turned and led the man back up toward the cabin and the cook fire in the yard.

"Oh, splendid! Colorado—we must be close."

"Close to what?"

"Why, listen, perhaps you could be so kind as to direct us to Massacre City." The man took out a clean white linen handkerchief and tucked it into his starched white shirt collar as he began to eat.

Brannon looked at the man. "Massacre City? Never heard of it. But I'm from Arizona and haven't spent much time in Colorado except right here."

"Well," Miller said sighing, "I'm afraid we're probably lost. And they said that there was a wagon road right up to the town."

"Does it take a wagon that big and four mules just to tote your gear?" Brannon asked.

"Oh, yes. A field camera weighs a good seventy pounds, and then there're the collodion plates, the silver nitrate, the glass plates, the darkroom, and the paper. Not to mention the fact that everyone now wants to see it in stereoscope. So there's a stereo camera, and . . . "

Miller stopped his discourse when he noticed that Gilmore had finished picketing the horses and was trudging up toward them. "Gilmore! Bring up a tin of crackers and one of peaches!"

Then, turning to Brannon, he offered, "May we add our share to this repast, sir?"

Brannon cracked a smile. "It would make a much more pleasant meal than beans and bread. You fellas help yourselves while I wash up and put on a shirt."

When Brannon returned, the other two were in the midst of a discussion that ended abruptly at his arrival.

"Oh, er . . . Gilmore here is my assistant. You are Mr. . . . "

"Brannon. Stuart Brannon."

"Mr. Bannock? We do thank you for your hospitality. Listen, we were just having a discussion," Miller continued. "Well, I suggested to Gilmore here that we take a photograph of you standing in front of your mine. It would be a keepsake for you, and I could use the print in one of my publications."

Suddenly Gilmore piped up, "But I told him that no man wants his diggin's exposed to the whole world."

Hawthorne H. Miller nodded at Gilmore. "Why, no man would pass up an opportunity to—"

"The boy's right."

"Right?" mumbled Miller.

Brannon pointed to Gilmore. "Is that your whole name?"

"Jeremiah Gilmore, but my friends call me Jeremy." The boy nodded.

Brannon returned the nod and then turned to Miller. "There won't be any photographs taken around here," he ordered. "I've had too much company already, present company excluded."

"Well, I certainly don't see how it could . . . " Miller pushed back his little helmet and peered into Brannon's piercing eyes. "However," he stammered, "that's certainly your choice."

"Tell me about Massacre City." Brannon eased the tension by changing the subject.

"Well, sir, it's a fascinating tale. I believe the story will do well, but a few photographs would certainly enhance reader interest. I presume you have not heard of the massacre?"

"I've been up in these mountains for about a year," Brannon admitted.

"Well, let me tell you a story of courage, bravery, hardship, and tragedy," Miller intoned. "I first heard about it in Santa Fe. This information, I might say, is completely reliable, for I secured it from eyewitnesses." The man stood to his feet and began to pace back and forth.

"Last winter in December, a party of prospectors left Tres Casas for the treasure fields on the Little Yellowjacket. Of course, that was before gold was discovered up there."

"So they did find gold! Charley Imhoff was right!" Brannon shouted.

"Oh my, yes. The Box Canyon Mine alone could be worth millions according to all reports. But, mind you, this party of adventurers were going merely on speculation. Anyway, in the party were several seasoned men and several immigrant families. I believe there were seven children in the group."

"I hear it was seventeen children," Jeremy Gilmore interrupted and was immediately silenced by Miller's glare.

"I have the story recorded, and I can assure you it was seven children. This party was trapped just over Brighton Pass by a severe winter snowstorm and avalanche. Several of the members perished in the storm. As the terrified group huddled for safety in the biting wind, they were savagely attacked by combined forces of Ute and Apaches. Those that weren't slaughtered were taken captive as white slaves by the tribe."

By now Hawthorne H. Miller was at his arm-waving, oratorical best. "Two wounded men were able to escape and find their way across Brighton Pass. These men, near death, stumbled into a hunting camp of one of the town's more prominent families and told their story just before they died. Well, the hunting party, several brothers actually, responded to the dastardly action as any true men of the West would. Putting aside their own safety and the needs of their families, they immediately plowed their way through the storm and up Brighton Pass to rescue the women and children from the wild men."

If Miller had not been so enthralled by his own declarations, he might have noticed that Brannon's steel gray gaze was slowly turning to fierce anger. Miller rambled on.

"Well, it seems the brothers caught up with the savages at a high mountain meadow. The leader of the murderous kidnappers turned out to be a half-breed squawman."

"A what!" Brannon growled.

"Oh, you know, a white who bought some wretched Indian woman for a wife."

Hawthorne H. Miller had spent his life trying to avoid conflict. He had no idea what to do when Stuart Brannon jumped to his feet. In fact, he seemed genuinely puzzled to see Brannon's bronzed and powerful right fist flying at his head.

He was unconscious before his body ever hit the ground.

Jeremiah Gilmore jumped to his feet. "What did you do that for?" he stammered.

"For insulting a lady, son." Brannon looked down at Miller. "He'll be all right in a minute."

"Insulting a lady?" Gilmore repeated. "You mean what he said about some squaw—"

The words were hardly out of his mouth before Brannon jerked the boy completely off his feet and held him by the collar. Brannon's right fist was clinched as tight as his teeth.

"I'm sorry, Mr. Brannon!" the boy cried.

Brannon lowered the boy to his feet. Jeremiah Gilmore found his knees couldn't hold him, and he dropped to the ground.

"Now," Brannon said with disciplined calm, "you tell me the rest of Mr. Miller's story."

"Yes, sir . . . uh . . . well uh, well, those brothers—"

"Were their names Rutherford?"

"Yes, sir, Mr. Brannon. Did you know them?"

"Go on with the story."

Gilmore gulped, then continued. "Well, as Mr. Miller tells it, the brothers confronted the squawman . . . I mean, the leader of the tribe, and he refused to release the white women and children, so a gun battle started. Just as the Rutherford brothers were gaining the upper hand, in rode about fifty more wild Indians, and they just slaughtered the whole party of rescuers right there in the meadow. I hear they mutilated the corpses and everything."

"Well," Brannon breathed deeply, trying to control his rage, "if everyone died, just how did this story get told?"

"One of the brothers, Dixon, had been wounded in an earlier battle and was told to stay back in the woods out of the way. He witnessed the whole scene from the mountaintop. Knowing there was nothing he could do by himself, he hobbled back into Tres Casas and told the story."

"Is that the whole account?" Brannon pressed.

"Well, sort of. But Dixon also reported that he had helped one of the white women escape, but she went crazy and refused to leave the cabin. He, being wounded and a gentleman, didn't want to force a woman to do anything against her will, so he gave up and left her there. That's why we're headed to Massacre City. Dixon Rutherford is there now." Gilmore gulped.

Brannon picked up the wash basin and tossed the contents on the head of a groping Hawthorne H. Miller. "Jeremy, I like you, so I'm going to tell you something. Don't you ever repeat that pack of lies to anyone on earth. There isn't a speck of truth in the whole story."

"You—you know what really happened?"

Miller was now trying to rise. Brannon put a foot on his chest and slammed him back to the ground, jamming his boot heel against Miller's rib cage.

"The Rutherford brothers were vicious killers. Anyone who's been in Tres Casas more than three months can tell you that. They caught up with Tristo Lanier's party in Brighton Pass and murdered several men. They probably had already killed the two that Lanier had sent back for help. Those that escaped made it to a cabin where Everett Davis and I were wintered out. It so happens that Harlan Rutherford had bought an Indian girl and treated her terribly. She sought asylum with us because she was hurt and was about to have a baby."

Miller mumbled something and squirmed under Brannon's boot. Brannon jammed the boot heel in deeper and continued to talk to Jeremy Gilmore, ignoring Miller's protests.

"Through the grace of God, two men and an Irish family made it to our cabin, and we helped barter back one of their children who had wandered into an Indian camp. It was then that the Rutherfords showed up demanding directions to a gold mine, whose owner they had already killed, and they threatened to further molest the Indian lady. We refused to allow such a thing to happen and fought it out with them.

"A very brave Frenchman lost his life, and the Indian lady would also have perished, except that her brother came by in time to kill her attacker. The lady who stayed at the cabin was Mrs. Mulroney, who was understandably distraught, but came through the ordeal well enough. She and her husband and three children were last heard to be running the station at Broken Arrow Crossing. Now, son, you know the real story."

"Broken Arrow Crossing? That's called Massacre City now," the boy exclaimed.

"Boy, you hitch up those mules as fast as you can while I try to keep from killing this snake under my boot!" Brannon shouted.

Jeremiah Gilmore seemed relieved to flee from the scene.

"My word, I've never been so insulted. The sheriff will certainly hear about this. No squawman can—"

With one motion Brannon lifted Hawthorne H. Miller to his feet and at the same time drew the Arkansas knife out of his boot.

"Miller, have you ever seen a man with his tongue cut out? Well, let me tell you it's a pitiful sight. He can't talk, he can't eat . . . just a slobbering, gurgling pathetic creature. The name of the lady you have been slandering is Elizabeth. She is a Nez Perce woman with dignity and honor. Neither I nor anyone else touched her while she was at Broken Arrow Crossing."

Shoving the stumbling Miller down to the wagon where the boy was hurriedly hitching the team, Brannon continued, "I want you to say, 'Elizabeth is a fine lady.'"

"You can't bully me. I'll have the sheriff—" Miller tripped as he stumbled on toward the wagon.

Brannon grabbed his collar once more and shoved the knife to the man's throat. "Miller, unless you plan on leaving your tongue lying here in the dirt, I want to hear you say, 'Elizabeth is a fine lady!'"

Jeremiah Gilmore was already in the wagon with reins in hand.

"Say it, Miller!" Brannon pressed.

"He'll do it, Mr. Miller, he really will!" Gilmore cried.

In a halting, low whisper, Miller muttered in a singsong fashion, "Elizabeth is a lady."

"Louder, Miller! A fine lady. Say it!" Brannon shouted.

With a panicked look in his eyes, Hawthorne H. Miller cried out, "Elizabeth is a fine lady!"

"Yes, she is, isn't she?" Brannon replied, releasing the photographer. "Miller, I promise you, if I see those lies in print, I will track you down and make you pay. If you want truth, you can get it from Edwin Fletcher or Everett Davis or Peter Mulroney. But don't you ever go to telling those lies.

"Now, get him out of here, Jeremiah. And take my advice, son, get a new job."

The wagon rumbled and squeaked back across the Trabajacito with Stuart Brannon watching its rapid departure.

When he turned back to the fire, Red Shirt was scraping out the last of the peaches. "Good food," he said smiling. "You know, I never seen man with tongue cut out."

Brannon breathed deeply and started to relax. "Neither have I," he said with a sigh. "Neither have I."

FOUR

Northwest winds rage across the mountains and funnel down the Trabajacito every day in September. The only times a stiff cold breeze does not blast a person's face are those quiet, serene moments between sundown and dark.

Stuart Brannon sat cross-legged, leaning back against the outside wall of the dugout cabin. Red coals glowed from the campfire only a few feet from where he sat. His Winchester rifle lay at his side. The small kerosene lantern hung on a peg near the door of the cabin, still unlit.

Brannon hardly noticed the brown hawk that dropped from the sky, sending a terrified pika back into its lair among the rocks and boulders of the mine entrance. His mind was consumed with the scratchings, numbers, and names scribbled on both sides of a scrap of wrapping paper that served as his ledger.

For over an hour he had been calculating the amount of timber, dynamite, drills, hammers, rail line, carts, steam engines, winches, pulleys, nails, foodstuff, tents, buildings, and manpower needed to properly develop the Little Stephen Mine.

Smelter! I haven't even thought about how to get it to a smelter! Brannon groaned. He knew the big money would come following the lode down into the ground, but all he knew about mining was what he had learned during the summer from Everett Davis. Most all of that concerned the finer points of placer digging.

Hard rock mining! We'll have to hire some mining engineer

from Europe. Maybe Fletcher knows someone. Fletcher? Where is he? And Davis? Everett should be here to make these plans.

Thoughts about Davis brought Brannon out of his daze and to his feet. He fluffed up the fire with a stick or two and walked away from the dugout toward the creek. For days he had tried to avoid thinking about Davis.

Everett won't desert his friends. He won't cat around and waste time. And he won't get lost. He's dead, in jail, or tied to a tree somewhere between here and town.

"I should have gone! It's only right. I should be the one to track down Everett. Brannon, the only reason you sent Fletcher is because you're afraid to leave this mine! Has the promise of riches done that to you?" Brannon mumbled to himself all the way to the creek.

He wasn't at all surprised to see Red Shirt and the other two Ute Indians come up to the creek from downhill.

"When the sun rises, you will have visitors," Red Shirt reported.

"How many?"

"Three men, no wagon."

"Bad men?"

"¿Quién sabe?" Red Shirt nodded. "One man wears a badge and carries two pistols. The second has been here before. He rides the big paint. I think maybe that will be my horse. And the third, he does not belong out here. He looks like a preacher."

"A preacher?" Brannon smiled. "What do you know about preachers?"

Red Shirt knelt by the water's edge and scooped up a drink. "A preacher once rode into our village."

"And what did you do?" Brannon quizzed.

"We ate his horse," Red Shirt replied, showing no emotion whatever. "He walked out. We invited him to return when he had a new horse, but he never came back."

"Well, there could be some trouble here," Brannon mused.

One of the other Indians spoke to Red Shirt. "He says, 'Will there be shooting?'"

Brannon stood broad-shouldered with his hands on his hips. "Perhaps." He nodded.

The Indian spoke again, this time waving his arms towards the creek.

Red Shirt added, "If there is shooting, we will stay in the trees and watch. Perhaps there is a horse we can find."

"Find?"

"You can't steal a dead man's horse, so we will wait and see if we find one."

"Well, thanks for the warning. Maybe there will be no shooting."

Red Shirt started to leave and then turned back. "If the Brannon dies tomorrow, we will come and eat his food."

Stuart Brannon spent the first half of the night plotting his defense. He barred the door shut on the dugout and then exited out the tunnel to the mine entrance. He rolled several large boulders in front of the entrance to make a barricade in case he needed to hold out at the mine. He carried the Winchester and two pistols on him at all times, with plenty of ammunition for each. He slept out behind the boulders that circled the little front yard of the cabin.

Dawn brought further preparations. Logs that had been dragged in for support timbers were stacked to form a crude wall on the far side of the tunnel entrance. They provided a place, other than the cabin and mine, behind which to hide. Brannon chewed on some cold, tough, salty jerky as he waited for an oncoming attack.

It was several hours later when they arrived. The three riders stopped on the far side of the creek and shouted towards the dugout.

"Brannon! This is Trevor. Listen, these two men have come to talk with you. We're going to cross the creek now, but we don't want a fight. What do you say, Brannon?"

"Stay on that side of the Trabajacito!" Brannon commanded.

"Look, Mister," the man with the badge shouted, "I'm Clifton

DuPrey, the sheriff down at Tres Casas. These men have a legal matter to settle with you, and I'm not about to stand in the creek shouting all day!"

The sheriff spurred his roan horse and started to splash across the stream. Brannon fired a warning shot into the tree above the rider's head, spooking the horse, causing it to spin in circles as the sheriff tried to keep from falling into the shallow water.

"Mr. Brannon," the one dressed as a preacher called. "Mr. Brannon, I'm Abner Cheney. We have a matter of prior grant deed to discuss with you. I know that Mr. Vance came in here and tried to scare you off, but that was a violation of my instructions. I have fired Waldo Vance. Now we've rode straight up to you. We didn't sneak in here. We do not intend to shoot at you. May we ride in and discuss this?"

"You and the sheriff can ride in. Trevor stays on that side of the creek. If there's not going to be any shooting like you said, then you won't need him," Brannon hollered back.

"A point well taken," Cheney returned. Then he and the sheriff came across the creek and rode up to the little yard in front of the dugout cabin.

Stuart Brannon, wearing his white deerskin shirt, stood up from behind the log barrier. The Winchester lay across the top log, still pointed towards the creek and Trevor, who had dismounted and tied his horse.

Brannon held his Colt in his right hand pointing it in the direction of Cheney and the sheriff. "I hope you boys will excuse my lack of hospitality, but I've been shot at and beat up several times in the past few weeks by people who claim to be associated with Abner Cheney. It makes a man jumpy. For instance, if Trevor crosses the creek, I'll be so nervous I'd probably gut-shoot you, Mr. Cheney. And if the man with the badge goes for his gun, the two of you will have to be satisfied to be buried in the same grave. So I'll just keep my guns out, and you keep yours tucked away."

"I assure you I don't carry a gun, Mr. Brannon," Abner Cheney said.

"Yeah, well, I once got shot in the back by a man who told me the same thing up in Abilene. So state your business and then trot on out of here."

"Mr. Brannon," Sheriff DuPrey began, "Mr. Cheney has got papers showing that the mineral rights to this whole mountain belong to him and the Colorado Southern Mining Company. You're trespassing on his claim."

"Mr. Cheney's a liar. Nobody's given that big of a claim and you know it, Sheriff."

"Mr. Brannon, the U.S. government made an agreement eight years ago that the Colorado Southern Mining Company would be given this mountain as partial compensation for building a railroad through this country," Cheney reported.

"He's got the papers here, Brannon." The sheriff broke in. "It was brought to my attention that you were up here illegally. Now Mr. Cheney realizes that you might not have known about his prior claim to the land. So, being a gentleman, he does not want to have you arrested. You just need to vacate the land."

"Actually, Mr. Brannon," Cheney added, "you may take whatever gold you have already dug. Frankly, I am amazed that you found much color here. My geological reports indicate that most of the gold will be found on the north slope of the mountain."

"Is that what you came to say?"

"Yesss, basically," Cheney stuttered.

"Well, I give you gents three minutes to cross the Trabajacito and ten minutes to be clear out of sight." He aimed his pistol straight at the sheriff.

"Now wait a minute, son, you can't threaten me; I'm a lawman!"

"Well, Mr. DuPrey, maybe you are . . . maybe you aren't. I have no way of knowing. The last time I was in Tres Casas they never had any laws—let alone a lawman. You could be some old trail bum that Cheney hired out of a saloon. Because you don't know much about law. Your jurisdiction is at Tres Casas, which happens to be in New Mexico Territory. This mountain is in the proud and sovereign state of Colorado. That badge is worthless out here."

"Except in the pursuit of a criminal who flees across a state line," the sheriff announced.

"I haven't been perfect," Brannon responded, "but as far as I know, I'm no fugitive from justice."

"I've got a complaint filed against you by Dixon Rutherford," the sheriff reported. "He claims you bushwhacked two men from Lanier's party on this side of Brighton Pass, and that makes the crime in my territory. He also claims that you back-shot and killed his brothers Harlan and Oake. But since that was up at Broken Arrow Crossing, it don't affect me."

"You believe Dixie Rutherford?" Brannon fired back.

"Didn't say I believed him; just got a complaint filed."

"Now, Mr. Brannon," Cheney added, "can't you see that the sheriff is willing to forget the whole matter if you just pack up and ride off?"

"Ride off to the north, that is," the sheriff insisted.

"Brannon, the sheriff is offering you a mighty good deal," Cheney rattled on.

"Well, sir, Mr. Cheney, I'm going to offer you a good deal. Instead of merely gut-shooting you, I'm just going to shoot you in both legs. Course you might spend the rest of your days a cripple, but you'll be alive. Does that sound like a good deal?"

"You're mad, Brannon!"

"Nope. You see, you fellas think you can chase me away from this claim. If I turned my back on my partners and myself, I'd be crippled in the head for the rest of my life. It's an offer I cannot accept. Good day, gentlemen." Brannon, using his pistol as a pointer, motioned for them to leave.

"Mr. Brannon," Cheney fumed, "I shall report this to the U.S. Marshall's office in Denver! You will not be allowed to keep this mine!"

"Cheney, you can report it directly to President 'Rud' Hayes for all I care. Some men can't be chased out, scared out, or bought out. By the laws of God and man, this mine belongs to us, and I'm a mighty stubborn fella when I know I'm right. So you just back on down the trail with your hired gunman and your hired sheriff. Go find some other poor working man to bully." Brannon pointed the pistol at Cheney's left leg and cocked the hammer, keeping his eyes constantly on the sheriff's gun hand.

Cheney yanked off his hat and wiped his brow with a white linen handkerchief. It was a cool day, but he was wet with sweat. He turned his horse and walked it back toward the creek. Sheriff DuPrey stared at Stuart Brannon.

"Brannon, if you cross that state line, I'll arrest you!" he growled.

"DuPrey, when I return to Tres Casas, I'll march into your office on my own. You make sure Dixon Rutherford is there waiting."

He watched from the barricade as Cheney and the sheriff recrossed the creek. They stopped on the far side and huddled with Trevor. Finally, Cheney yelled back at Brannon, "How far does this claim of yours stretch, Brannon?"

"All the way to the creek."

"Good, then I'm sure you won't mind if Trevor camps out over here. He would enjoy watching the progress of your operation."

Brannon hunkered down behind the logs and watched as the sheriff and Cheney rode south. Trevor pulled the saddle off his horse and settled in by the trees. It was a situation Brannon had not anticipated.

Mines are never in the right place. He's got the trees and the water. Every move I make will be in plain sight!

He replaced his gun in his holster and pushed his hat to the back of his head. Leaning against the boulders near the mine entrance, he could watch Trevor and still have the protection of the log barricade.

He's not carrying a rifle, and a pistol would be useless at that distance. Maybe he'll wait it out until dark and then make a move. But if he wanted to move on me, he could have done it last time. The others might be going around to the far side of the mountain. Or maybe they are going to the U.S. Marshall's office. They left him here just to keep me pinned in! They aim to arrest me, not just chase me off!

Stuart Brannon thought of himself as a peaceful man. He had to be deliberately prodded to enter a conflict. But he knew how to fight. His earliest memory, and about the only one he had of his father, was when he was ten years old and had challenged three big teenage bullies on the streets of San Antonio.

He had been beaten black and blue, but he was still swinging when his father had pulled him out of the pile of boys and demanded a explanation.

"They pushed Kori Saylor and made her cry!" he had tried to explain. "It ain't right; they shouldn't have done that!"

"It *isn't* right," his father had corrected him.

That's it. That's all he had said about the fight.

It's okay to fight for what's right, only use the proper grammar when describing it.

Stuart Brannon had been in and out of fights ever since. Almost every time he fought for what was right and fair. And almost every time, he won.

Lord, the idea crossed my mind to just go ahead and shoot this Trevor, but for the life of me I can't figure out how I'd explain it to You . . . or Lisa. I can handle a fight, but an armed wait isn't exactly my strength.

Trevor settled down, sitting on the ground, leaning against a tree with his hat pulled low. Brannon could not tell if his eyes were open or closed.

Brannon spent the entire day with one eye on Trevor. That meant staying outside the cabin and mine, patching up a few tools, rearranging the barricades, stirring up the fire—but mostly just planning.

By sunset, he had decided on his course of action. He let the fire burn down to a faint glimmer by the time it grew dark. Then, working as silently as his bare feet would allow, he made camp ready for the night. Propping a fifty-pound sack of flour against the outside cabin wall, he pulled his white shirt over the flour sack. A couple of rolled blankets formed the "legs" of the sitting decoy. Then he topped it with his hat and laid an empty shotgun across the "legs."

Brannon shrugged at the charade. "Well, ol' boy, you don't look like much, but maybe you'll give me a margin," he mumbled under his breath.

He pulled on his torn coat and left his boots crammed on the end of the rolled blankets. Then with a rope slung over his shoulder, a Colt in his right hand, and another pistol tucked into his trousers, he moved slowly on hands and knees toward the trees upstream from where Trevor was camped.

Using the red glow from Trevor's fire as a guide, Brannon slipped across the mountain, always staying low so that no silhouette could be seen. By now the night air had turned chilly as the winds began to stir. His feet and toes felt numb. Yet he pushed on, one step at a time.

Moving, waiting, watching . . . moving, waiting, watching.

Once he heard a rattle of leaves in the distance, but he could still see Trevor hovering around his little fire. Brannon reached the creek fifty yards above Trevor. He rolled up the legs of his trousers, found a small stick about the size of his thumb and bit down on it. Then, crouching low, he began to wade across the frigid waters of Trabajacito Creek.

Every step was painful and slick.

When he reached the far side, Brannon sat down quickly and began rubbing his feet. Finally, as the circulation increased, he started toward Trevor's firelight. He knew that the greatest danger was that he might startle the horse.

Brannon moved even more slowly than before, inching from tree to boulder to bush to tree. It wasn't much of a plan, but he had no intention of trying to work a mine under the eye of a professional gunman.

Besides, Fletcher and Davis should be pullin' in by tomorrow night at the latest! I don't aim on them stumbling into an ambush. So Brannon figured he would get the jump on Trevor, disarm him, hogtie him to the saddle, if need be, and send him back down the mountain. It was the disarming part that was unclear. Brannon knew Trevor would never surrender his weapons without a struggle.

In that way he and Trevor were alike.

It wasn't the best of all plans, but it kept him from a grinding anxiety about Davis and Fletcher. Brannon knew that if they didn't return in the next couple of days, he would have to abandon the claim anyway and begin a search on his own.

Lord, I'm a cattleman—who doesn't own a single head. I'm a native of the plains . . . and I'm stuck up here in the mountains. I'm most comfortable on horseback, and here I am crawling barefoot in the dirt. I don't even want to be here. Look, I'll take care of Trevor—and, please, You take care of Davis and Fletcher.

Trevor had picketed his horse downstream in what was left of a little meadow. Brannon could see the horse in the shadows dozing off while still on its feet. Trevor was leaning against a tree, asleep. But Brannon pushed on with the assumption that the gunman might be awake.

Coming up straight behind him, Brannon crept silently through the pine needles and leaves, his confidence growing since the gunman had not even twitched or spat. The night lights of a skinny moon were almost completely blocked by the foliage of the trees.

Brannon acted by the dim reflection of the dying fire and by instinct. He reached the back side of the tree and muffled the sound of his gun cocking with his coat. Then with the Colt aimed at the back of Trevor's hat, he reached around slowly and lifted the rifle from the man's lap. Brannon held his breath and pulled the Winchester to his side. Then slowly standing to his feet, Brannon pointed the pistol at the back of Trevor's head.

"Time to turn out, Trevor." He shoved the pistol barrel into the back of the man's hat.

Trevor didn't flinch.

"I said move it!" He poked again at Trevor. This time the gunman's head tumbled to the ground.

At that moment, Brannon suddenly dove to the dirt and rolled back to the trees. "Of course!" he scolded himself. "He set up a decoy, too!"

With both guns drawn and his eyes searching the darkened countryside, he glanced back at the bedroll that had moments before looked so much like a gunman in the shadows.

He could be anywhere in the trees! And I walked right into it!

Brannon lay still for a moment waiting for Trevor to make his move. *Come on . . . do something . . . step on a twig . . . shoot . . . say something!*

Suddenly the breezy night air was shattered by a piercing scream and a loud string of curses coming from behind the mine.

Brannon stood to his feet. "The traps! Trevor was sneaking up on me and got into a trap!"

He scooped up Trevor's rifle and splashed across the creek, stumbling in the darkness of the night. Breaking into his own camp, Brannon pulled on his white deerskin shirt, shoved his boots on his wet and freezing feet, and replaced his hat.

"Brannon, get up here and get me out of this thing!" The words were mingled with pain and panic.

Brannon lit the kerosene lamp and walked cautiously up the hill behind the mine, with pistol drawn, searching the shadows for the injured Trevor.

Maybe's he's trying to sucker me up here, Brannon thought.

He wasn't.

Even in the flickering light Brannon spotted Trevor trying furiously to release the pressure of the bone-crushing trap on his bloody, mangled foot.

The gunman looked up quickly at the oncoming kerosene lantern, his face flushed white. Without saying a word, he suddenly crumpled to the ground, passing out from the loss of blood and shock.

Brannon made a quick check for weapons and found Trevor's pistol tossed to the ground. Then he set the lantern down, bent to his knees, and with great effort forced the jaws of the trap open, releasing Trevor's foot. Struggling to keep his balance, he pulled the wounded man to his shoulders and carried him back down the mountain to the dugout cabin. Leaving the unconscious gunman by the fire, Brannon recrossed the creek and brought Trevor's horse, tack, and bedroll to the mine.

After pulling off the mangled boot, he took an empty grub sack from Trevor's warbag and wrapped the gunman's injured foot. He carried the gunman into the dugout, laid him on the plank-board bed that served as Fletcher's bunk, and tied his hands to the bedposts. Then, after removing anything that resembled a weapon from the room, Brannon went outside to the fire.

He was startled but not surprised to see Red Shirt and his friends sitting silently next to the glowing coals.

"Is he dead?" Red shirt asked.

"Nope . . . just chewed up a bit."

One of the braves spoke in Ute, and Red Shirt translated. "He wants to know if you are going to eat the man."

"Eat him?"

"Well, you trapped him. When you trap something, you either use it for food or for hide. That thin white skin doesn't make a good hide, so you must be—"

"No! I'm not eating him!" Brannon interrupted.

"Good, then we stay for dinner. How about the horse? Want to trade the horse for something?"

"It's not my horse," Brannon insisted.

"Yes. Your horse. Captured man cannot own horse," Red Shirt informed him.

"We don't do things that way," Brannon replied.

"You could learn." Red Shirt smiled and nodded to the other two Utes. "Besides, the Brannon needs what we have to trade."

"What do I need?"

"Help in fighting the bad men."

"More? There are more coming?"

"Maybe twenty-five or so."

"When?"

"Maybe two days . . . maybe tomorrow."

"What direction are they coming from?"

Red Shirt got up and sorted through the pots on Brannon's fire. "They come from the waterfalls. One has been here before."

"Cheney? The one that looks like a preacher?"

"No, little man with round hat."

"Vance? He's coming back?"

"He and many friends. So you give us the pony, and we might help you fight."

"It's not my horse," Brannon insisted.

"Where's the man?"

"In the cabin," Brannon answered.

Red Shirt got up and walked to the cabin. He flung the door open and shut without looking inside.

"The man say it's okay to borrow his horse."

"Wait a minute!" Brannon protested.

"If the man gets well, we bring back horse." Red Shirt pulled up the picket pin and started to lead the paint horse away.

Brannon fired a shot into the air, and all three Indians stopped instantly. "You're not taking the horse, Red Shirt!"

The expressionless Indian turned back to the fire. "How about beans? We will stay and eat the beans then."

"You're welcome to 'em," Brannon said sighing.

FIVE

wenty-five to one is a tinhorn bet. If I could get Vance by himself...

Brannon decided at daybreak he would pack up all the guns and ammunition he could carry and head straight at the oncoming invaders.

Either I'll find a place to isolate Vance ... or ... or I'll just duck them and go look for Fletcher and Davis.

Abandoning the mine was the last thing he had thought he'd ever consider. His conscience could only be soothed by the fact that he still had a few hours to figure out another plan.

But by daylight, Brannon was still staring into the coals of the fire. He went in and untied Trevor and helped him hobble out to the fire and breakfast.

"It'll turn gangrene," Trevor moaned.

"Maybe." Brannon nodded.

"Look, push me up on my horse, and I'll ride out of here to see a doctor," Trevor begged.

"You've rode away before, and yet you keep coming back. Here's what I'll do—I'll fill you full of grub and then tie you to that tree."

"You can't leave me tied to a tree!"

"I could leave you with a bear trap on your foot. Anyway, if I don't come back, yore ol' buddy Waldo Vance will show up and release you."

"Are you kidding? If Vance finds me tied to a tree, he'll shoot me."

Brannon nodded. "Well, he didn't take a liking to your walking out on a fight."

"I don't walk away from any fight," Trevor growled. "Being on the same side as Waldo Vance is like shooting yourself in the leg. That's why Abner Cheney fired him."

"If Vance isn't working for Cheney, who is he working for?"

Trevor finished drinking his coffee. "I suppose he's crazy enough to think he could muscle his way in and take over the Little Stephen on his own."

"Well, Trevor, you better pray that I survive. It might be your only hope."

"I wouldn't pray for you, Brannon, if hell froze over."

"Suit yourself. Say, I should mention that your first visitors will be three Ute Indians. Just tell Red Shirt to help himself to the beans."

"Utes? Brannon, you can't do this to me!"

"Trevor, you've got a mighty mean reputation. It seems like all sorts of folks end up with bullets in the back whenever you're in the neighborhood. Well, I don't intend on being one. So you just sit tight and be nice to the visitors."

Brannon didn't bother listening to the curses as he left.

Pulling his frayed jacket over his deerskin shirt, Brannon buckled down his own saddle on Trevor's paint horse. The descent down the Trabajacito Creek canyon was peaceful.

The steady hoofbeats of the horse, the constant trickle and splash of the creek, and the soft rustle of aspen leaves in the wind were the only sounds he could hear. In the last few days the trees had begun to change colors. Fog-gray moss hung down from the dark green fir trees. Little spruce seedlings clustered along the trail like puppies anxious for affection. The giant groves of aspen reflecting yellow and burnt red looked like a patchwork quilt on the mountainside.

Somewhere down below, Brannon knew the Trabajacito tumbled off a thirty-foot cliff and splashed into the Rio La Plata. And somewhere down there, men rode hard with intent to kill him.

He half expected to meet Red Shirt and friends on the trail, but they were nowhere in sight. Brannon stopped when the sun was high and dug into the grub bag he carried. He had enough food for dinner and supper. After that he figured to be back to camp or dead.

It was late afternoon before he spotted a cloud of dust far down the canyon revealing a number of riders headed his way. Brannon supposed they had just climbed the steep rocky arroyo behind the Trabajacito waterfall. He moved off the narrow trail and now pushed the paint through the thick brush on the east side of the creek. Coming upon a small box canyon, Brannon calculated that this would be the best place for a group to bed down for the night.

Working the horse slowly up the crumbling granite slope at the back of the canyon, he finally reached the rimrock. He tied the horse to a greasewood bush and then settled in behind some boulders at the edge.

Well, at least I can tell who's headed my way.

Brannon still didn't have a plan. "If they keep going, I'll just slip on down to Tres Casas and look for the others. If they camp . . . well, maybe there's a way," he mumbled.

He sat in the shadows and waited.

Waited until the breeze turned cold.

Waited until the sun turned dusty orange on the far western horizon.

Waited until one rider, then a second, then a string of riders came out of the cottonwoods and cedars and broke into the clearing at the opening of the box canyon.

The third man on the trail wore a round bowler, and even in the dusky light Brannon immediately recognized Waldo Vance. The other men were unrecognizable—not because Brannon was too far away, but rather because they looked like all other men in the West—dust-covered, shabbily dressed, tired, their faces reflecting years of chasing dreams that turned out to be mirages.

"Fletcher!" Brannon choked to hold back his shout.

Toward the rear of the string three horses were being led by one man and guarded by two others. On the first horse sat Edwin Fletcher with his hands tied behind his back. Then came a pack horse. *Undoubtedly our supplies!* Brannon moaned. And on the third guarded horse rode a woman in a dark blue dress, awkwardly sprawled across the saddle.

A woman! Fletcher was down in Tres Casas with a woman? No wonder he took so long! No wonder he slipped up and got captured. Where's Everett?

Instantly, the entire plan changed.

Caution and wisdom and years on the trail advised Stuart Brannon to wait until it was darker before he made a move. But something in his gut told him he had better act fast. There was no way to lead the horse down the rock canyon quietly, so he left the paint tethered and began easing down the granite ledge a step at a time. He had a knife strapped in his boot, one pistol in his holster, another in his belt, and the Winchester in his right hand.

Tattered black hat pulled low, Brannon crept from one rock to another. By the time he reached the floor of the canyon, the posse had turned their horses loose to graze and had set up camp out near the trail where guards could survey the situation both upstream and down.

They're just taking a supper break! Nice of them to leave the mounts all saddled up.

The grazing horses and dimming twilight provided sufficient cover for Brannon to slip up near the boulders just outside the campfire. About half of the men were cleaning guns, but the others huddled around Fletcher, the woman, and Waldo Vance.

Lying behind a fallen rotting tree trunk, Brannon listened in on the conversation.

"I say, you'll have the devil to pay if you touch her!" Fletcher shouted.

Brannon could tell by the bruises across Fletcher's face that it wasn't the first stand that he had made that day.

"If you're trying to scare us about Stuart Brannon," Vance sneered, "forget it. He doesn't have a chance against this troop."

The woman held onto Fletcher's roped arm and looked down at the ground.

She could be a reckless twenty-five or a gracious thirty-five.

Whoever she is, she's with Fletcher, and I'll have to pull them both out of the fire.

Her black hair streaked with a fine line of gray was pulled behind her ears. Her face, when she turned it in Brannon's direction, revealed a bronze hardness—a few deep lines from years of tough times. Yet, there was a reflection about her that let him know this had been a beautiful woman. In the palaces of Europe or the big mansions of New York bankers, she could have still turned heads and dominated conversation. She was one of those women who defies age.

She's scared, Brannon thought, *but she's been through it before. She'll fight. She'll fight them tooth and nail.*

Waldo Vance dominated the conversation. "Look, nobody touches the woman or the Englishman until we get Brannon! We're too close now to lose all that gold."

"How about after we kill him?" one of the men growled. "Then we take care of her, right?"

Fletcher interrupted. "Kill Brannon? It's been tried before."

"Well, it can't be that tough!"

"Tell that to the Rutherford brothers." Fletcher fought for words and time.

"He was the old boy who leaded them down?"

"Quite."

"That doesn't matter!" Vance insisted. "No man can take on twenty-one men!"

Twenty-one? That's better than twenty-five—sort of.

"Men," Fletcher continued, "I guarantee you that Stuart Brannon will take several men with him when he goes. Just which of you plan on dying so that these others can divide up the gold?"

"Ain't none of us have to die. Mr. Vance has a plan."

"Well, I certainly hope he hasn't told you that Brannon will give himself up just because you captured me. The last time someone was held hostage, Brannon shot the hostage."

"That's a lie," Vance protested.

Fletcher, this better be leading somewhere!

"You should have seen him at Broken Arrow Crossing!"

"Vance, you didn't tell us that Massacre City gang was up in these mountains," a man toward the back shouted.

"Gang?" Waldo Vance yelled. "It's just one man!"

"If there's only one man, why did you need twenty-one men?" Fletcher quizzed.

"I been wondering that myself," one of the men added.

"That's enough," shouted Vance. "Tie them up and put them over there by that log." He pointed in Brannon's direction. "I want two guards on them at all times. And don't start worrying about Stuart Brannon. He's a ladies' man. I could tell it. All we have to do is just drag her out in the clearing and slap her down a couple of times, and Brannon will fall all over himself trying to rescue her. I know the type, you wait and see."

Fletcher didn't reply.

Why on earth did you bring a woman up here!

Brannon rolled back away from the log and made it into the brush before Fletcher and the woman were shoved to the ground on the far side of the log. The two guards perched on a stump across from the bound couple. One proceeded to clean his revolver while the other rolled himself a quirly.

As a plan started to come together in Brannon's mind, he sorted his way through the darkness back out to the middle of the box canyon to the horses. Using a strip of rawhide off his shirt for a halter string, he slipped alongside the horse Fletcher had been riding and pulled the rawhide around the horse's neck. Then he slowly led the horse to the back of the canyon near the ledge that he had ascended earlier in the day, and he tied the horse to a greasewood.

He knew that the horse could easily pull loose if frightened, but he hoped it just might stand there if all was quiet. Brannon immediately turned back and found their pack horse, which had been unloaded, and led it to the place where he had tied Fletcher's horse. It took him the better part of an hour to find the third horse, the one the woman had been riding. This time he tied the horse in the middle of the box canyon and then crept back up to where Fletcher and the woman were guarded.

As long as he stayed behind the log, he could remain out of the flickering light of the guard's campfire. But there was no way to pull Fletcher and the woman out and not start a gunfight.

So it was a matter of waiting.

Brannon waited for one of the guards to wander back to the main fire.

Or doze off.

Or . . . something.

It might have been moments . . . or hours . . . but Brannon found his mind bouncing from gold to fortunes to cattle ranches to Lisa and the baby to two stone tablets that marked the part of the ranch where his wife and child were buried.

That's why I'm here, Lord. For the ranch. I'm going to use this money to build the nicest little cattle ranch in Arizona. Then I'll put two polished marble markers, You know the kind, with the cross on the top, right out there on the graves. And I'll build a white picket fence around them and plant some rose bushes.

Suddenly he wished it were daylight. He wanted to pull out the locket and look again at Lisa's face—her smile, her eyes, her hair!

Movement by one of the guards brought him out of his daydream. The man stood up and stepped back into the trees.

Brannon moved lightly and quickly. The barrel of his pistol slammed into the back of the remaining guard's head before he even looked up.

Fletcher sat straight up and started to speak, but Brannon dove toward the couple and quickly silenced him. Without a word he dragged the unconscious guard behind the log and returned wearing the man's hat. He pulled a blanket around his shoulders and waited for the second guard to come back.

"Say, Logan, did you hear a noise just now?" the guard mumbled as he slid down next to Brannon.

With startling speed, Brannon whipped out his Colt and stuck the barrel right into the guard's stammering mouth.

"Unless you plan on your brains decorating the back of that box canyon, you better keep quiet—understand?" Brannon whispered. "Now untie those two very slowly!"

Brannon never took the gun barrel out of the frightened man's mouth. The guard fumbled with the ropes, finally releasing

Fletcher, who quickly undid the woman's bonds, whispering to her as he did.

Brannon motioned to Fletcher to tie the man up and then pulled off the man's dirty bandana and stuffed it into his mouth, rolling him over the log and on top of the other guard. Still without a word, he motioned for Fletcher and the woman to follow him back into the box canyon. When they reached the horse tethered in the middle of the canyon, Brannon pulled them close and whispered, "Edwin, we've got to get out in a hurry. Why on earth did you bring this woman out here?"

"Look, Brannon, I'm delighted to see you. There's no easy way to say this . . . Stuart, Everett Davis is dead. This is Velvet Davis. She's Everett's sister!"

"Dead?" Brannon's mind bounced wildly. "Sister? Everett doesn't have a sister in Colorado! He can't be dead! Dead? How?"

"Do we have time to talk, or should we get out of here first?" Fletcher challenged.

Brannon felt a shortness of breath, a sinking feeling in the pit of his stomach, and his mind and eyes began to blur. He heard his well-rehearsed instructions rattle off his lips, giving no indication of his heart.

"Go straight to the back of this canyon. The horses should be tethered to a bush. Grab them and wait until you hear a commotion. Then lead them up the granite ledge. It's steep, but keep going, you can make it. Up on top you'll find a paint tied up."

"Trevor's paint?" Fletcher quizzed. "My word, did you kill him?"

"Not yet," Brannon whispered.

"And where will you be?" Velvet Davis asked.

"I'm going to run these horses right out the canyon and over the camp. Then I'll lope up here. In the dark they won't think anyone can make it out the back side of this canyon. We should have until daylight to make it to the mine."

Fletcher and Miss Davis scooted into the darkness towards the granite wall at the back of the canyon. At the same time, Brannon swung into the saddle of the other horse and began to slip around behind the horses, most of which huddled together near the mouth of the canyon.

Figuring that he had given Fletcher and Miss Davis time to reach the back of the canyon, Brannon spurred the horse straight into the herd of milling horses, firing several shots from the Winchester over their heads.

As he expected, the horses bolted for the creek and the familiar trail, right over the top of the camp full of Vance's men. Shouts and shots exploded in every direction, frightening the horses even more. Brannon spun his mount and loped through the dark for the back of the canyon. Sliding off his horse, he led the nervous buckskin up the ledge in the dark.

It was too dark to worry about sliding off the canyon wall. He reached the top exhausted and wringing with sweat. Fletcher and Miss Davis stood there waiting for him.

"There's no paint, Stuart," Fletcher reported. "But the saddle's piled here on the ground."

"Red Shirt!"

"Who?" Miss Davis asked.

"A Ute Indian. He wanted that horse. You ride this horse, and I'll saddle the pack horse."

Brannon took the lead across the top of the mesa with the other two close behind.

"Dead? Everett's really dead?"

"Looks like he was bushwhacked on his way to the courthouse on the edge of Parrott City."

"Everett made it to my house," Miss Davis offered. "He was shot up pretty bad. The doctor said he'd never make it through the night. But he held on for two weeks. Davises are tough, you know."

"Everett never once mentioned a sister. I asked him about family, and he mentioned a brother in trouble with the law down in Yuma, but no sister."

"Well, he certainly talked a lot about you, Mr. Brannon. I know about last winter and Elizabeth and Littlefoot and Fletcher and Trudeaux. All about the Mulroney family, the Rutherford brothers. And I know about the Little Stephen Mine."

"Velvet filed all the papers for us, including Everett's sworn statement giving his share of the mine to her," Fletcher added.

"To her . . . to a woman called Velvet? Lady, what's your real name?"

"Velvet Davis," she huffed.

"Ma'am, let's start this again. What is your name?"

"Brannon, I must protest—" Fletcher began.

"Edwin, if you're telling me I have to share the gold mine with a new partner, then I'm entitled to know her real name. What's written on that so-called sworn statement?"

"Corrie," she whispered. "But everyone calls me Velvet. The rest is true. Everett left me his part of the mine."

"My word, Edwin, how do we know she didn't kill the old man herself?"

"Well, the statement was witnessed by Dr. Flynn. Naturally, I assumed—"

"Did you talk to this doctor?" Brannon quizzed.

"Well, not actually, but I did—"

"Great! I don't even know if Everett's dead. Did you see the body?"

There was a long silence.

"Fletcher, how naive can you get? How do we know—"

Fletcher cut Brannon short. "Stuart, look, I don't know what's eating at you and why you insist on tearing down this lady even before you know anything about her. I not only saw Everett dead, I wrapped him in a blanket, carried him down the street, and laid him in a box. I set him in a hole and threw the dirt over him!"

Brannon did not look up.

"Then I recited the Lord's Prayer and read over him from his own Bible!" Fletcher yanked the tattered Bible from his coat pocket and slapped it in Brannon's hand.

Stunned, Brannon didn't speak for several moments. He didn't bother wiping the tears that streamed down his cheeks.

"I'm sorry, Edwin," he stammered. "I . . . I just didn't want to believe it."

"It's quite understandable," Fletcher murmured.

"Maybe, but not excusable. Look, Corrie, I mean Velvet, let me start this all over. I just don't handle death too well."

"I know," she said softly. "Everett told me about your baby and your Lisa."

"Well, I have a tendency to lose everyone I ever cared about. It's a major miracle that Fletcher has lasted so long."

Miss Davis looked Brannon in the eye. "My fiance was shot in the head by a stray bullet as I got off the stage in Denver after I had traveled across the country to marry him. I was left on the street, not knowing a soul and with five dollars in my purse. Frankly, Mr. Brannon, I haven't had three good days since then."

Brannon led them off the back side of the mesa. They crossed the main trail and splashed across the Trabajacito. "How about starting from the beginning?" Brannon asked. "When did Everett make it to your house?"

"It was Monday, the tenth of September. I was renting a little—"

"What's the date now?"

"Why, I believe it's Thursday, the fourth of October," Miss Davis answered.

"October? Did you hear that, Fletcher? It's October already!"

She continued, "I live on the outskirts of town. I was taking in washing, ironing, and such. When Everett reached my door, I hardly recognized him. He took two shots in the back, one in the shoulder and one in his right leg."

"His back! He took it in the back again?"

"I laid him, blood and all, on my sofa and ran to get Dr. Flynn. He dressed up the shoulder and leg wounds, but he said the bullets in the back were too deep to dig out. He said that Everett would die by daylight, so I just tried to keep him quiet and comfortable."

"And he lived for two more weeks?"

"Yes. I was by his side the whole time. He would pass out and then come to. When he was awake, he was always talking."

"That's Everett."

"Usually he would wake up quoting Scriptures."

"'I'm going away to prepare a place for you' . . . right?" Brannon smiled.

"Yes, and Psalms . . . "

Brannon nodded. "He really liked the Psalms."

"He said you were a man who was afraid of nothing but the will of God. Mr. Brannon, why did he say that?"

"Everett said that? Why, that old man nags at me from the grave. Who shot him?"

"No one knows," she said softly. "Everett said he had never seen the man before. Just a drifter, he thought."

"Who went after the bushwhacker?"

"You mean," she asked hesitantly, "like a lawman or posse or something?"

"Yeah, who's chasing the killer?"

"No one, I presume. They didn't know who to look for. Really, what can be done?"

"Justice!" Brannon snapped. "Justice, Miss Velvet Davis, that's what can be done!"

The three went single file through a narrow gorge, and then they pushed the horses up the rocky bank.

"You must be quite a bit younger than Everett," Brannon restarted the conversation.

"Oh, yes. But he was only fifty-two. Twenty-nine years of prospecting took its toll."

"And the war—that probably aged him," Brannon added.

"I'm sure it did," she agreed. "Everett always had plenty of stories about his time with the . . . uh, Illinois regiment."

"Well, Miss Velvet, whatever your name is," Brannon said as he pulled up the reins on his horse, "let's set the record straight. Everett Davis was from Michigan, not Illinois, and you're not his sister! So just who are you, lady?"

Fletcher stiffened. "Brannon, your impertinence can be . . . "

For a moment she sat silently looking down at the horse's mane.

"He's right, Mr. Fletcher. Look, I'm not his sister, but everything else is the truth. Everett Davis signed the claim over to me, as I said. My Christian name is truly Corrie Davis. But we're not related. When he told me his name, well, it sort of gave me the idea."

"So why the charade?" Fletcher quizzed.

"Because, Mr. Fletcher, I do not have a history of being treated fairly by men. Most are about as cynical and hard as Mr. Brannon. You two wouldn't have even listened to me if I had told the truth."

"Touché, Brannon," Fletcher said with a sigh.

"That kind of thing won't hold up in court," Brannon announced. "I mean, you butter up an old man on his deathbed just to get him to turn over his money, then—"

In the moon shadow of the trees along the creek, Brannon never saw the knotted reins flying through the night until they stung his cheek.

"Good show, Velvet," Fletcher commended.

"Look," Brannon finally said, "I was out of line. We'll settle up this matter about the claim later on. If we don't come up with a plan to ward off Vance and that gang of men, we won't be around to fight over the gold."

Brannon carefully explained the situation at the mine, including the visit from Cheney, the sheriff, and Trevor.

"You left Trevor tied to a tree?" Fletcher questioned.

"It was either that or shoot him," Brannon concluded.

"What if he gets loose?"

"He won't go far on a bum foot without a horse. Besides, there's more to worry about from Vance right at the moment. When they get those horses rounded up, they'll start up this trail madder than ever."

"Then you do have a plan?" Fletcher asked.

"Sure. You shoot ten of them, I'll shoot ten of them, and Miss Velvet here can shoot the other one."

"Really, Brannon! I do wish you had more respect for the lady."

"It's all right, Mr. Fletcher," Velvet Davis assured him. "Out here we're expected to pull our own weight. If it comes to defending our claim to the mine, you can count on me, Mr. Brannon. I can handle a Winchester, but I prefer a double-barreled shotgun."

"My word!" Fletcher gasped.

"I sort of figured you for that, Miss . . . eh, what is your name again?"

"Look, I told you my legal name is Corrie Davis, okay? But I've been going by Velvet Wendell for so long, I'd prefer using that name. I understand changing one's name is not a rarity out here."

"Nope. Wendell it will be," he said with a sigh.

Brannon pulled his hat low and spurred his horse forward.

The dark eastern sky had turned gray when they reached the crossing of the Trabajacito near the mine. Suddenly, Red Shirt rode straight toward them on the paint horse.

"Red Shirt? Nice horse! You didn't bother telling me you were taking the horse." Brannon smiled.

"I left your saddle. I do that only for the Brannon. Besides, it's not your horse," Red Shirt added. "Bear Man gave me the horse."

"Bear man?"

"Stuck his foot in bear trap, so we call him Bear Man."

"He gave you the horse?"

"We traded."

"And what did you give him?"

"Ropes."

"You let him loose?"

"Yes. We thought the other men would kill you anyway."

"Thanks."

"Maybe they will today," Red Shirt replied. "It does not look good for the Brannon."

"Yes, well, I know, twenty-one men are on their way."

"And some are in the mine already."

"In the mine? Who?"

"Bear Man, the preacher, and two more."

"Preacher?" exclaimed Fletcher.

"Cheney. He means Abner Cheney. Everybody wants in on the gold mine." Brannon stood in the stirrups and looked hard through the trees at the entrance to the Little Stephen Mine.

"Not the Utes," contended Red Shirt. "But we will wait in the forest. I think there will be many horses to find today."

Red Shirt rode out of sight, leaving Brannon and the others staring like outsiders at their mine.

S I X

On some other day, in some other decade, some other season, the upper reaches of the Trabajacito Creek canyon would have been a pleasant place for a picnic. The deep blue sky acted as summer's final curtain—warm days and comfortable weather. A fat mountain bluebird caught Brannon's eyes as it swooped down at the creek and then lit on a branch hanging over the tumbling water.

Stuart Brannon stepped down from the horse and slowly loosened the cinch. "Well . . . let's sit here and figure this one out," he suggested.

Edwin Fletcher and Velvet Wendell followed Brannon's lead and dismounted. The thick brush and the clumps of cottonwood, aspen, and spruce blocked the view from the dugout cabin and tunnel entrance.

"I say, Brannon," Fletcher interrupted, "what is the plan for getting them out of there?"

"Well, to tell you the truth, I was thinking about taking a nap," Brannon replied.

"What? We're going to let them take over our mine?" Velvet Wendell stammered.

"Our mine?" Brannon led his horse further away from the creek. "Look, as I see it, we have two enemies. There's Cheney, Trevor, and who knows how many more holed up in the mine. Not a lot of men, but they have a good defensive position."

"And then there's Waldo Vance and gang," Fletcher added.

"Exactly. Now if we get caught in a cross-fire between those two, we won't have any chance at all."

Fletcher tied his horse to some bushes, and then sat down next to Brannon. "So you think we should just wait it out?"

"Well, if Waldo is on his own and made big promises to those men, then he's not about to go along with Cheney or anyone else."

"My word, do you mean let them fight each other over our mine?"

"And we could just wait until it's all over," Velvet Wendell exclaimed.

"That thought did cross my mind." Brannon nodded.

"That should thin out the strength on both sides," Fletcher advised.

"Well, there's just one drawback." Brannon shrugged. "If for some reason Vance and Cheney decide to team up, they got the mine and a small army to guard it. There would be no way to regain possession."

"We do have the papers," Velvet Wendell replied.

"Yeah, and Cheney has papers. Probably Vance himself has some papers. What we need at the moment is possession."

"So there will be no naps?" Fletcher asked.

"Not long ones, anyway."

"I thought as much. Brannon doesn't often sit around and watch someone else fight his battles," Fletcher said to Velvet Wendell.

"Why don't we attack them both at the same time?" she questioned.

Brannon laughed. "Well, Fletcher, she has spunk. Actually, I thought we'd pick a side, make sure it wins, and then worry about the next step."

"What? Pick sides? Brannon, are you mad?" Fletcher demanded.

"No . . . " Velvet Wendell said hesitantly. "It does make sense. If our joining in on the fight helps one side win, then they would owe us something."

"But it's our mine to begin with!" Fletcher pulled his hat off and ran his fingers through his hair.

"Well, then, let's go get it back!" Brannon stood up and grabbed the reins of his horse. All three tightened up their saddles and remounted.

"Now, Brannon, you do know what you're doing?" Fletcher cautioned.

"Yeah, just like that time Elizabeth and I walked out into the meadow to face down the Rutherfords."

"At Massacre City!" Velvet Wendell cried out.

"I say . . . Massacre what?" Fletcher mumbled.

"Broken Arrow Crossing seems to have gained a new name," Brannon informed him.

"But the story Everett Davis told me sounded nothing like the tales of Massacre City, so naturally I assumed they were two different places."

"Miss, I'll tell you what. Don't you believe everything you hear about me," Brannon proposed, "and I won't believe everything I hear about you."

Brannon crossed the stream and stopped the horses at the distant side of the clearing leading up to the dugout and mine. With rifle laying across his lap, he called, "Cheney! Step out here and talk."

Suddenly Trevor appeared at the tunnel entrance. "Looks like you're trespassing on company property," he shouted.

Abner Cheney came to the door with a man wearing a badge by his side. Then another man filed out of the little cabin.

"Brannon, we would appreciate your vacating the premises. If you'd like to lay claim to personal belongings, I'm sure we could accommodate that," Cheney shouted. "This is U.S. Marshall Shelby Rosser. He has jurisdiction here, you know."

"Howdy, Marshall," Brannon called. "I'm glad to see you here. I've got papers too, and that's our mine you're standing in. You can help us settle the matter a bit later. But that's not what I wanted to talk to you about."

"What do you want, Brannon?" Trevor shouted.

"Trevor, I'm not talking to the hired help. I'm talking to Abner Cheney. I just thought we'd offer you our services. Twenty-one

armed men are riding hard to this mine and plan on killing anyone defending it."

"Yeah, and the Apaches want to move to Chicago and sell
doughnuts," Trevor gruffed.

"Look," Brannon yelled, "I'll make this quite clear. We're
going to be back up the far side of that hill. About the time you
figure you've lost the battle, all you have to do is shove one of
those snowshoes out the gun slot, and we'll hit them from the
back side."

"This is absurd, Brannon!" Cheney yelled.

"Listen carefully! I'm not going to repeat it. If we come in here
and save your hides, then you will have to walk away from this
mine."

"Brannon, this is U.S. Marshall Rosser. Your threats are bor-
dering on criminal activity."

"Marshall, have you ever killed twenty-one armed and dangerous men at one time?"

"Of course not!"

"Well," Brannon continued, "you and your deputy better get
ready to. Cheney won't pack iron, and Trevor can't hit a man
unless he turns his back."

At that word, Trevor went for his pistol. Even though the shot
was ineffective at that range, Brannon returned fire from the
Winchester.

Trevor turned to dive back into the mine, but twisted his bad
ankle causing him to collapse on the dirt. Hurriedly he crawled
back into the mine. Brannon didn't bother firing another shot.

"If someone does show up," Cheney replied, "who shall I look
for?"

"Your old buddy, Waldo Vance, and about twenty back-alley
cronies. He's not too happy about the way you cut him out of this
deal. I suppose he'll want to shoot you himself."

"Vance? You want me to worry about Vance?" Cheney
laughed. "I can handle him with a twenty-dollar gold piece."

"Not this time, Cheney. We'll wait. When you're ready, just signal."

Brannon turned and led Fletcher and Wendell back across the

Trabajacito. He stopped the little group on the mountainside where the trees thinned out and then stationed them behind the boulders with a good view of the clearing and the creek.

"How can we be sure that Vance and Cheney won't settle their differences without gunfire?" Fletcher pressed.

"Well, that's where Mr. Greed will just have to help us out," Brannon suggested. "He seldom fails."

"So we are just going to wait it out up here?" Velvet asked.

"No, not just wait. I think I'll take that nap." Brannon settled in between a couple of boulders and pulled his hat low over his eyes. "Edwin, you're on guard. Let me know when Vance and the others start up the arroyo."

Brannon knew that the length of their wait depended upon the time it had taken Vance's troops to round up the horses and whether they could find the trail in the dark. Fletcher watched the creek. Velvet pulled off her lace-up boots and rubbed her sore feet.

Stuart Brannon closed one eye, but with the other studied Miss Velvet Wendell.

Nerve. She's either dumber than a sheep or one brassy woman. How on earth could she believe she could waltz in here and demand a share of the gold mine!

"Mr. Brannon?" Her words startled him.

He sat up quickly, causing his hat to tumble forward. "Yes, ma'am? I must have nodded off."

"Mr. Brannon, you were staring at me from under that hat brim. A woman certainly knows when a man is staring at her!"

"Well, don't take it personal, Miss, eh, Velvet. See, I don't even know what name to call you."

"Mr. Brannon, I couldn't care less what you call me in private. I doubt if you could think of a name that some man hasn't called me previously. However, even though my given name is Corrie Davis, I would prefer your calling me Velvet Wendell when we are in company. Eighteen months ago I was working at a cafe in Denver when a man named Nobby Leone busted into the kitchen, stole the cash box, and shot and killed the owner, Mr. Brackentein. Leone didn't know I had witnessed the whole thing. Well, I testified against him in court, and he was sentenced to hang. The only problem was that he escaped and went on a drunken rage through town threatening to kill me."

She turned to look straight at Brannon. "So a couple of friends at the cafe chipped in some money and put me on a stage going south out of Denver. It got me as far as the shacks of Parrott City, and that's where I've been stuck ever since. I took the name Velvet Wendell to try to keep hidden from Nobby Leone. And since I have to take care of myself, I would greatly appreciate it if you and Mr. Fletcher call me Velvet Wendell in public."

Brannon stared at her blue eyes for a minute. "That's the first thing you said that makes sense. Velvet Wendell it is then. Even so, I still can't figure you out. Either you think we're a couple of country boys that you can hustle. Or . . . you really did talk Everett Davis into giving you a share of the mine."

"And you can't figure out which?"

Brannon replaced his hat. "I can't figure why an old-timer like Davis would give away his fortune to the first woman he meets. I mean, you're young enough to be his . . . "

"Daughter?" She finished the sentence. "Thanks, Mr. Brannon. Actually, I'm thirty-two years old and some days much, much older. Colorado hasn't been an easy place for a woman alone who refuses to crawl into some gold-rush cribhouse."

"That's fair enough," Brannon admitted. "I shouldn't have been so nosy." He laid back down and pulled his hat completely over his eyes.

"As for why Everett Davis wanted to give me an interest in a gold mine, I suppose it was just kindness for kindness. I knew him long enough to find out he was a man of Biblical principle."

"Well, you're right about that," Brannon agreed. "But trading a ton of gold for two weeks' nursin' . . . you've got to admit it was high pay."

"I didn't do it for pay, Mr. Brannon! I did it for free, and Everett Davis knew it. He was dying, and he didn't have anyone else to leave it to. You already had a share. At that point I don't think he cared about anything except making sure all his accounts were paid down here on earth. So he was generous with me because I was generous with him. No, I don't suppose that makes sense to someone as gold hungry as you are. It just seemed to Mr. Davis to be the decent thing to do. You know, Stuart Brannon, you keep wondering if Everett judged me wrong. Well, I've been wondering if maybe he judged you wrong. 'That Brannon's a fine Christian man,' he would tell me. But I've not seen too much to convince me yet."

Her words stung Stuart Brannon's conscience. He felt shallow and petty.

"Brannon! Here they come," Fletcher called out.

Velvet Wendell quickly began to replace her shoes.

"Okay, now look. When they get to the clearing, Fletcher and I will sneak down into position behind Vance and his men. When you see Cheney signal for help, Miss Velvet, you fire a warning shot from that double-barrel, and Fletcher and I will take that as a sign to begin."

"Begin what?" Fletcher pressed.

"We'll pin them down, maybe put the clamps on Vance, and get some of them to turn back."

"And the rest?" Fletcher asked.

Brannon took a deep breath and sighed. "That will be up to them."

For the first time in his life Waldo Vance felt in control of his own destiny—and he liked the feeling.

He no longer had to whimper, "Yes, Mr. Cheney."

He no longer had to cower before the threats of hired guns like Trevor.

He was the captain of his own fate.

A general of his own army.

And no one could stop him now.

Even his hostages' escape was not a setback in his mind. After all, the plan had been hatched before the chance encounter that ended in their capture. Most of the men knew only that they would reestablish Vance's legal right to the mine. He had forged a beautiful set of papers to convince them. Tres Casas had been swarming with drifters looking for easy work. He had no trouble rounding up a crew at one silver dollar a day.

Actually, Waldo Vance was considering keeping them on to maintain the peace in all his ventures. They might just build a town next to the mine. "Vance City" had a certain ring to it, in his mind.

Most men never get a chance to make it big, he thought.

This was his chance. He would not let it escape his grasp. The plan was quite simple—surround the mine and starve them, burn them, or shoot them out. To guarantee the men's loyalty, all who stayed on with him would receive a bonus in gold.

Stuart Brannon troubled Vance only in that he knew the man would fight to the death. *Totally inflexible,* Vance thought.

Vance was considering the feasibility of putting in a toll road between the soon-to-be-his gold mine and the new diggings up at Silverton when he approached the creek crossing at the Little Stephen Mine.

Gathering the men close, "General" Waldo made his appeal.

"I believe there are no more than three or four people holed up in that cabin or in the mine. Perhaps one of them is the woman. I want to give them time to surrender and leave the property. That's why I brought so many of you up here. If they refuse to do so, we will have to force them out. I would rather avoid bloodshed, but these are dangerous and violent people, and I expect at least one of them to fire on us.

"Don't take unnecessary chances. If we have to wait to burn or starve them out, we will do that." Then with a noble air, he continued, "There is a remote chance that some of us will get hurt. In fact, as leader I could be the very one to take a bullet. If so, I must know that I've settled things fairly with each of you. I want to pay you now for this day's work in advance, just in case I'm not here when the shooting stops."

Vance magnanimously handed each man his pay.

In reality, he had no intention of getting in the line of fire. With twenty blazing guns, his would not be needed or missed.

"Men, I'll see if I can call them out. Hold your fire until I give a signal." Then he shouted at the mine entrance, "Brannon, I want to talk to you!"

From the rocks behind Waldo Vance, Stuart Brannon watched and waited to see if Cheney and Vance would wind up being allies or enemies. It didn't take long.

Brannon saw Marshall Rosser open the door to the cabin to answer Vance's challenge. Immediately "General" Waldo's lack of command was evident when one of his men nervously pulled off several rounds that slammed into the cabin wall. The marshall dove back inside.

Trevor, appearing at the mine entrance with rifle in hand, fired one shot that struck Vance's wild gunman right above the belt, dropping him in the dirt of the La Plata Mountains. Men scattered anywhere they could find shelter.

Several dozen shots thudded against the cabin and around the mine entrance. Those inside returned the fire, allowing Brannon and Fletcher to move undetected into position closer to Vance's troops.

So many shots began to ricochet off the rocks at the tunnel entrance that Trevor dove out of the mine and behind the log barrier Brannon had built.

Two of Vance's men took low to the brush and began to flank the cabin and circle up the mountain behind Trevor. As shot after shot continued to fly in both directions without any damage, Brannon watched the two men inch their way up the mountain. They stopped by one of the large boulders he had rolled into place. Then one took a step forward.

The ear-piercing scream of pain when the trap snapped closed caused gunmen on both sides to stop shooting for a moment.

All except Trevor. He rolled to his right, whipped around, and shot the man caught in the trap. The other man, surprised to see who was behind the logs, shouted, "Trevor, it's me, Smokey!"

The words had hardly left his mouth when Trevor pulled off two more rounds, and Smokey tumbled to the ground without firing a shot.

One of Vance's men turned back to him and shouted, "You didn't tell us that Trevor was on Brannon's side."

Vance struggled to find an answer. "He's not on Brannon's side!" Vance hollered. "I don't know why he's here!"

At that point the deputy dove out the cabin door and took a position behind the big boulders circling the cabin's front yard.

"Trevor," Vance screamed, "what are you doing up there?"

"Trying to save my life from sheep dip like you, Waldo!" came the reply.

"You're a dead man, Trevor. We've got you outnumbered!"

"If they're all as gutless as you, Waldo, we have nothing to worry about!" Trevor yelled.

Several shots flew in Trevor's direction causing him to duck low behind the barrier. The deputy leaned over a rock and fired three times, bringing down a gunman in the woods. But at the same moment a barrage of lead flew back across the clearing, and the deputy dropped flat to the dirt for protection.

"Trevor!" Vance shouted again, "I got nothing against you. Send out Brannon!"

"This property belongs to Colorado Southern. Cheney, a U.S. marshall, and his deputy are here," Trevor yelled. "You boys will all be arrested for attempting to kill a U.S. marshall."

Suddenly some of the men began to question their leader.

"Vance, you told us there were claim jumpers up here."

"Yeah, you didn't tell us about no marshall!"

"I ain't going up again' Trevor!"

"Nobody going to arrest me for tryin' to kill a marshall!"

"Wait! Quiet!" Vance cautioned. Gathering up courage, he ran towards the edge of the clearing.

"Trevor, you liar! If Cheney is in there, send him out!"

Suddenly the door to the cabin cracked open. Brannon couldn't see who was there, but he recognized the voice.

"Vance, you idiot! You'll be hanged for this!"

"Mr. Cheney! Are you in there?" Even in his moment of dominance, Waldo Vance sounded like a clerk.

He cleared his voice and then spoke again. "Cheney, I've got as much claim to this mine as you do and you know it! We'll let you men ride out of here. We just want Brannon and this mine. No man will stop me!"

"Under what authority?" the marshall called out.

"Under the authority of twenty-one well-armed men!" Waldo shouted.

"About seventeen!" Trevor corrected. "At least three are dead and you don't count."

"Vance, tell your men to hold their fire. Let's you and me meet and settle this matter without shooting anyone else."

There was nothing Stuart Brannon could do but watch and listen from the sidelines as the two men came together in the clearing between the creek and the mine.

Waldo Vance knew that what happened in the next few moments would set the stage for the rest of his life. He could not buckle under now. He would have to show his superiority. This time he, not Cheney, would prevail.

Abner Cheney marched up to Vance and shouted in his face, "What is the meaning of this? I fired you two weeks ago. You were nothing but a lousy clerk then, and you're a lousy, unemployed clerk now. This property belongs to the Colorado Southern Mining Corporation. It's being protected by the government of the United States. Now, Vance, I'd suggest—"

Waldo Vance was a man who had just been pushed over the line of reason. He hadn't planned on doing it. It was the pressure of the moment that seemed to dictate it.

"Call me Mr. Vance," he insisted.

"What?" cried Cheney.

"I said, from now on you will call me *Mister* Vance!"

"I don't recognize saloon scum as Mister," Cheney retorted.

Stuart Brannon had heard none of the words, but he didn't miss any of the action. Waldo Vance suddenly pulled a small revolver out of his coat pocket and waved it as Cheney screamed something.

A blast of smoke and flame shot from Vance's pistol, and Cheney fell back on the dirt. Waldo panicked into retreat, and bullets flew from every possible direction. Brannon hunched low to avoid any possibility of a ricochet. The front door of the little cabin was blasted from its leather hinges, and it crashed out into the yard.

Suddenly a deafening shotgun blast from high on the far mountain startled and silenced the gunmen for a moment.

The signal. The marshall's asking for help.

Brannon and Fletcher fired several quick rounds above the heads of the men gathered around Vance, and the whole party dove for new cover that would protect them on both sides. Trevor and the marshall returned fire, keeping those in the middle flat on the ground and unable to shoot. Waiting for leadership, most of them hesitated to fire in any direction.

"Men," Brannon shouted, "you are now surrounded. If you will holster your guns, walk slowly to your horses, and ride south back to Tres Casas, you will not be pursued."

"Brannon!" Vance was in hysterics. "Brannon, what are you doing out there? It's Brannon, men, shoot him! Shoot him!"

"If any choose to stay and live through this, you will be tried for participating in the murder of Abner Cheney!" Brannon noticed one man start to leave.

"You can't leave, get back here!" Vance screamed. He dropped his pistol in the dirt, then clutched it up, and waved it at the man. Suddenly a rifle barrel cracked across Vance's raised shoulder causing him again to drop his weapon. Several other men scooted down the hill for the horses.

"How do we know you got us surrounded?" one of the men shouted. Suddenly a volley of fire from Fletcher's direction sent the questioner diving for the dirt.

"Wait," he yelled, "wait!" When the shooting stopped, he got on his hands and knees and crawled to his horse. Several other men followed.

Vance tried to rally the troops. "Don't leave! What about the gold! Look, I'll give you a double bonus! Fifty dollars per man!"

Suddenly Waldo Vance started running right in Brannon's direction firing his gun wildly. One of his own men reached out and tripped him with his rifle. Vance whipped around on his hands and knees to view his assailant only to catch the stock of the rifle in the side of the head. He sprawled unconscious in the dirt.

"Mr. Brannon," the man who had silenced Vance now said, "Waldo here ran into a little trouble and cain't do no more talkin'. If we leave him here, can we ride out?"

"You ride south into New Mexico," Brannon yelled. "If one of you men ever comes north of Sleeping Ute Mountain, you'll be arrested. Do you understand?"

"Yes, sir."

"Then get out of here and get out quick!" Brannon yelled.

Guarding their positions, Vance's men sprinted from tree to tree to their horses to make their exit. Brannon kept his position until he was sure that all the men rode out of sight down the dusty trail along the Trabajacito.

The marshall ran out of the cabin to check on Abner Cheney.

"Fletcher, throw a rope around Waldo Vance. I don't want him coming to and crawling like a snake to cover," Brannon called. Then he headed toward the marshall.

"How's Cheney?" he asked.

"Still alive . . . barely," the marshall replied. "We should have taken your help earlier."

"Gold. It turns a paradise into a graveyard. None of these men needed to die!" Brannon sighed.

Trevor walked over by the marshall and Cheney. "He's losing a lot of blood! Can you help me get him up to the cabin?"

Suddenly Brannon's rifle came down off his shoulder, and he pointed it straight at Trevor.

"Marshall Rosser," Brannon barked, "we had a deal. You will abandon this site, correct?"

"My word, yes," the marshall interjected, "but we need to help Mr. Cheney."

"Yeah, you can carry him to our cabin. Maybe Miss Velvet can help. Edwin, where is she?"

Fletcher bounded up the far side of the mountain towards the rocks where Velvet had fired the shotgun.

Brannon had just helped settle Abner Cheney into the cabin

when he heard Fletcher yell, "Stuart! She's been hurt! Help me get her across the river!"

Stuart Brannon did not want to abandon his claim again. If he went to help Fletcher, then Trevor, the marshall, a deputy, and a wounded Cheney would be in the cabin, and he and the others stuck across the Trabajacito. Indecision ruled his mind.

"Brannon, get over here!" Fletcher yelled again.

Lord! What has this done to me?

He sprinted to the creek, splashed across the water, and grabbed up the limp woman from Fletcher.

"Edwin, what happened?"

"I figure she must have been knocked off the rocks by the recoil of that shotgun. Probably banged her head."

"She didn't have to pull both triggers!"

"Well, it worked, didn't it?" Fletcher insisted.

"Yep. It worked." Brannon turned back to the cabin. "Edwin, you catch the horses and bring them over. We might have need for them soon."

She's a little heavier than Lisa, he thought. *About like Elizabeth when she was pregnant.*

Since the cabin was already crowded with men, he laid her in the small yard near the fire circle.

I wonder how Lisa would have looked at age thirty-two.

Then he sorted through the cabin for another wash basin.

SEVEN

Early Spanish explorations such as those by Juan de Rivera and the Dominguez-Escalante expedition sprinkled their heritage and culture across the mountains and rivers of southwest Colorado. Stuart Brannon was halfway between El Rio de las Ánimas Perdidas and El Rio de Nuestra Senora de las Dolores. High up in El Rio de Plata canyon, on a tributary called the Trabajacito, Stuart Brannon now found himself surrounded by both lost souls and sorrows.

The tightness across her mouth and even the strained lines around Velvet Wendell's eyes seemed to relax as she lay unconscious in the little yard by the cabin.

There's a lady that has spent most of her life just trying to survive, Brannon thought. *She hasn't been dealt many good hands, but she won't toss them in without a fight.*

He pulled off his beat-up black hat and sighed deeply. Brushing back his tangled dark brown hair, he ran a dirty finger along the side of his own face.

Well, Miss Velvet Wendell, you and I are two of a kind. There haven't been a lot of years, just a lot of tough trails. We both look like we were rode hard and put away wet.

It was one of those fleeting moments to sit back and contemplate—a time to reassess the future, change goals, settle the mind back on the important things of life. It was a time to contemplate the purpose of one's existence, a chance to talk to God, to seek His direction.

That's what Stuart Brannon wanted to do.

But he didn't.

The moment wasn't long enough.

Fletcher had brought the horses in and was checking on the others in the cabin.

"Brannon," Fletcher called, "take a look at this wound of Cheney's."

There was work to do.

Pushing through the door, he began to give orders.

"Marshall, could you go drag Waldo Vance in here where we can keep an eye on him?"

Trevor limped over to Brannon. "I'd be happy to see that he never bothers another soul," he sneered.

"Yeah, that's what I figured." Brannon turned to the marshall. "I presume you want to take Vance in for trial?"

"That I do, son, that I do."

"Trevor, you and Deputy—"

"Gideon Giles," the young man offered.

"Well, you and Giles grab some picks and shovels out of the mine and go halfway down to the creek and start digging graves."

Trevor bristled at the suggestion. "Let the buzzards feast."

"Every man on earth deserves to have a proper buryin'," Brannon insisted. "Most of those old boys had no idea what this fight was all about. Besides, you two can keep an eye on the trail in case one of Vance's volunteers wants to double back and take a potshot."

"Where's the wound?" He stepped to Cheney's side.

"Well," Fletcher explained, "he's what you call . . . intestine, I mean, eh—"

"He's gut-shot," Brannon exclaimed. "Can't you just say it straight out?"

"It's rather crude," Fletcher protested.

"Edwin, you are living in a crude world, and Colorado is filled with crude people, and that, sir, is a crude and vulgar wound!"

"A point well taken," Fletcher conceded. "How serious do you think it is?"

"Well, at that range the bullet passed right through the body, but we don't know what happened on the inside. If he punctured a kidney or something like that, he just won't last long. Pour a little vinegar in that wound and wrap him tight to stop the bleeding. Make sure he gets some water, and then we'll just have to wait and see."

Brannon took a chipped enameled tin bowl outside and walked down to the creek. After washing his own face and swirling the bowl clean, he scooped up a couple of quarts of water and brought them back to the campsite. Edwin Fletcher was looking after Velvet Wendell who was still unconscious.

"Edwin," Brannon suggested, "take this water and wash her face. Maybe that will bring her around."

"Me? But . . . but," Fletcher protested, "you're our amateur doctor."

"Look at it this way, Edwin. When she comes to, who would she rather be looking at? An English gentleman, or some driftin' cowhand?"

"At the moment," Fletcher retorted, "both choices seem equally bad." He washed her face.

By evening, the Little Stephen looked more like a hospital than a gold mine. Cheney lay on a rough-hewn wooden bed that neither Brannon nor Fletcher had yet had a chance to use. The president of Southern Colorado Mining Corporation hung on to life by the thinnest of threads.

Velvet Wendell came to and couldn't remember firing the shotgun at all. She remembered seeing the signal from the marshall and then suddenly waking in front of the cabin with unshaven Edwin Fletcher staring into her eyes.

Trevor sulked around camp, mainly keeping to himself. It was obvious to all that whatever financially lucrative deal he had established would be lost if Cheney died.

At first they had taken the hogtied Waldo Vance into the mine to incarcerate him, but his screams and curses just magnified and echoed through the tunnel. So they tied him to the log barrier at the side of the mine and gagged him with his white handkerchief.

They took turns sitting by Cheney, and the others gathered around the campfire outside the cabin. The night air was bitter cold, and the moonless sky revealed stars that looked close enough to touch.

"Brannon," Marshall Rosser said, "Giles and me will be headin' out in the morning. We'll take Vance with us and lock him up in Denver. But that doesn't settle up the claim."

"Look, Marshall," Brannon added, "we discovered the gold, developed the mine, and filed papers on it. As I see it, the only claim Cheney has is if he ever put a railroad in up to Lake City. You and I know that won't happen until Chief Ouray agrees to move the Utes south. So I say the mine should remain ours until the courts can prove it otherwise."

"I have a tendency to agree with you, son—but don't underestimate the legal power of a man like Cheney. Local laws, state regulations, even federal mandates can get brushed aside when men with power begin to force the issue. Now as far as I'm concerned, you won't be seeing me up here again. Got no time for it. But Cheney's likely to bring the army with him next time. Sometimes you just cain't beat 'em."

"I can. I'm right this time, and I know it."

"But right don't always win in this world."

"You don't believe that, Marshall."

"It's true."

"But you and I don't believe it, do we?" Brannon asserted. "What's right has got to win . . . it's what validates our position. Without that we'd both be fools."

"Yeah, that's what we got to hold on to . . . but sometimes, Brannon, there's a mighty slick grip."

"Marshall, you notify Cheney's people about his condition. Has he got kin?"

"A nephew back east, I believe."

"No wife or kids or nothing?"

"Nope. Just married to his job and making money!"

"Well, at least the company knows he's here. He needs some medical attention."

"Maybe you could take him down across the La Plata Valley into Tres Casas. It's a cinch he can't make it back to Denver," the marshall added. "It's a rough ride across the mountains."

"I suppose someone could try to carry him down, but I'm not sure he'd live through it," Brannon commented.

"Ain't nobody taking Cheney anywhere without me," Trevor insisted. "I've got a bigger stake in keeping him alive than any of you."

"You're right about that," Brannon said nodding, "and you need to have someone look at that foot of yours."

"I ain't forgot how that happened, Brannon. You won't see the last of me until we settle that score."

"In the meantime, if Cheney dies, you're going to have a tough time settling up with him, aren't you, Trevor?"

"Cheney won't be riding," Deputy Giles reminded them. "How could you take him anywhere?"

Brannon stood up next to the fire. "We've got the horses. I suppose we could swing a stretcher between a couple of cayuses, but Trevor would need help with him, since he's banged up just a tad himself."

"I ain't travelin' with you," Trevor insisted. "You're just looking for an excuse to kill me and Cheney both."

"Look, Trevor, I don't lose a dime if Cheney croaks up here on the mountain or down in town or if he lives. But you're right about one thing, none of us are very thrilled about leaving the Little Stephen. Every time we walk across the Trabajacito, someone jumps our claim."

"I could go with them, Marshall," Deputy Giles offered. "I mean, you wouldn't really need my help with Vance."

The marshall rubbed the stubble on his face. "Yep, I suppose you're right."

Suddenly Velvet Wendell, who had been sitting and staring at the fire all evening, stood up and began to walk through the night towards the creek.

"Miss Wendell, where are you going?" Brannon jumped up to run after her.

"Why, I have to find my shotgun. I must have dropped it during the confusion."

"You remember!" Fletcher shouted. "My word, Brannon, her memory's coming back."

"Miss Velvet . . . we, eh, brought the gun in with you. It's all right, come on and sit down."

"No," she insisted, "I think I'll go to sleep now." Without another word, Velvet lay down in the dirt and immediately passed out.

"Fletcher, drag out Everett's buffalo robe. Let's just roll her up and let her sleep by the fire."

Within minutes and without planning, everyone settled into a place for the night. Trevor took over watching Cheney inside the cabin. Deputy Giles parked next to the log barrier so that he could watch Vance. Marshall Rosser fell asleep leaning against the cabin wall. Fletcher chose to be next to Miss Wendell so he could keep the fire going through the night.

Stuart Brannon didn't sleep at all.

He walked around the campfire.

He stirred the coals and added more sticks.

He carried some water back from the creek.

He boiled another pot of coffee.

He scooped up an armful of firewood.

He checked on the horses.

He checked on Cheney.

He checked on Vance.

Lord, men have died because of this gold mine, and we haven't even got to blasting out the lode yet. Maybe it would be a good idea if You reminded me of what's important. Life used to be simple . . . raise cattle, take them to market . . . then you raise more cattle.

Twice during the night Brannon walked down to the horses and considered throwing a saddle on one of them and just riding off.

Down to Parrott City to search for Everett Davis's killer.

Down to Arizona.

Down to the ranch.

Down to Texas.

With his head propped up on the slick leather seat of his old Visalia saddle, a dusty Navajo saddle blanket over his chest concealing his drawn Colt in his right hand, beside the dozing, picketed horses, Stuart Brannon finally fell asleep.

The sound was so soft, Brannon didn't bother opening his eyes. It could have been a breeze on the leaves. Like a brush of a soft broom on a clean wooden floor. No more than a swat of a horse's tail chasing flies on a hot summer day.

It isn't summer.

It isn't day.

Sleeping horses don't swat flies.

In the pitch dark they only swat . . . trouble!

Immediately his eyes popped open, but he didn't move a muscle. He could make out the shadows of the horses, but one seemed to have six legs. Purposely making noise, he cocked the hammer of his .44.

"Red Shirt, that horse is not lost!" he blurted out.

Showing neither fear nor surprise, Red Shirt and his two companions came out from among the horses.

"Why is the Brannon sleeping with the horses?" he asked.

"Because there are those who would sneak in the night and try to take what doesn't belong to them." He lowered the gun and placed it back in the holster.

"I am glad the Brannon is awake. We want to make a trade."

Brannon stood to his feet and stretched out his arms and legs. In the east, the hint of dawn began to gray the black night sky. "What exactly do you want to trade?"

"We want two more horses. You put some men in the ground; now you have many horses."

"What do you have to trade for them?"

"We will show you where there is another mountain with yellow stones."

"Yeah, that's just what I need, another gold mine!"

"It is near an old town of abandoned spirits," Red Shirt insisted.

"Abandoned spirits?"

"Yes . . . the ancient ones. It is down on the mesas. But we are not afraid."

"No more prospecting for me," Brannon insisted.

One of the other men spoke to Red Shirt, and then he interpreted.

"He says to give you one people wagon for two horses."

"People wagon?"

"Yes," Red Shirt said smiling. "Stagecoach!"

"You have a stagecoach?"

"Yes, we found it in the canyons—but is a little broken," he said nodding.

"Let's have some hot coffee and talk about it." Brannon motioned toward the fading coals of the fire up by the cabin.

"We will eat with the Brannon," Red Shirt said softly, "but we will not eat with the others. Some of the Brannon's friends are not good men."

"And some are not my friends," Brannon added.

The Indians quickly built a small fire by the creek, and Brannon retrieved the coffeepot and cups from the bigger blaze. After coffee and cold biscuits, the conversation started up again. Brannon, with his deerskin pullover shirt and sun-bronzed skin, looked strangely like the other men around the fire.

"It is getting cold," Red Shirt blurted out.

"Soon it will snow," Brannon offered.

"We must go and hunt," Red Shirt continued. "We need two more horses. We could take them, but then we would have to kill the Brannon."

One brave offered words of counsel that were quickly translated by Red Shirt.

"He says we have many men who hate us now; we do not need more enemies."

"This morning," Brannon began, "three men will leave camp going south. One is hurt. I want you to follow them for three days, then return, and tell me what you saw."

"And you will give us two horses?"

"No. Also, today there will be two men going east. A lawman and a bad man with a round hat. I want you to follow them for three days and then come back here and report to me."

Red Shirt interpreted the offer to the others. Then he turned to Brannon and asked, "We get horses after we report?"

"You get the horses right now!"

Red Shirt and the others clapped their hands above their heads and their faces broke into wide grins.

"We want the sorrel with—"

"You will take the horses I give you," Brannon declared.

"Yes," Red Shirt agreed, "we will take the horses you give us."

Brannon walked around the dozen picketed horses with the Indians trailing him. Because of the men who had died in the gunfight, several horses were unclaimed.

"These are the 'found' horses . . . " Brannon started. "That buckskin looks pretty well galled, and the black is favoring his white foot, so I'll trade you the sorrel and the Appaloosa," he offered.

"The Brannon is good friend! You did not give us the old horses!" Red Shirt smiled.

"I want you to be able to ride back and report to me." Brannon took careful note of the physical markings of each horse.

Red Shirt's companions immediately pulled themselves up on the two horses. The one on the sorrel jerked the horse's head to the right and instantly found himself in the middle of a blowout. The horse bucked high, then twisted to the left, spun right, and brought all four legs off the ground at once.

The mounted Indian flew over the top of the horse and crashed, shoulders first, into the brush alongside the creek, still holding a handful of mane. The bucking horse sprinted down the creek, spinning and kicking. Red Shirt and the other Indian doubled over in laughter as their slightly limping friend pulled himself out of the weeds and brush.

"Do you want one of those other horses?" Brannon asked.

"No!" Red Shirt shouted. "The horse it is very good. It is the rider who is poor!"

The other Indian, still mounted, spoke and Red Shirt interpreted. "He said, 'How does the Brannon know we will keep our word? Maybe we will just ride off to the canyons.'"

"Tell him, if he does not come back to report, the Brannon will follow him with a loaded gun."

When the words were repeated, all three Indians stared at him for a minute. Then Brannon broke the silence. "Besides, if you

don't come back, where will you go to eat beans for breakfast?"
He smiled.

Their somber expressions instantly broke into smiles.

"We will come back. You will save us beans and bread?" Red
Shirt asked.

"You will be welcome at my fire." Brannon tipped his hat to
the Indians who scurried down the creek to find the bucking
horse.

He kicked the small fire dead and then hiked back to the yard
in front of the cabin. Even though the sun was not quite up yet,
there was plenty of daylight. Fletcher had stirred up the fire, and
Trevor took the coffeepot from Brannon's hand and poured himself a cup.

"You givin' away horses to Indians?" Trevor mumbled.

"Well, now, it seems to me you made a deal with them over a
horse," Brannon said nodding.

"I owe you one for that one, too, Brannon," Trevor growled.

"Anytime you want to collect, Trevor, just make sure I can see
you face to face."

"What do you mean by that? Do you think I'm afraid of you?"

Brannon ignored Trevor's probes, which only made the gunman angrier.

"Fletcher, I traded those two horses away. If anyone comes up
to claim them, we'll pay them twenty-five for the sorrel and
twenty for the Appaloosa. We won't even charge them for boarding the horses."

"Do you really think anyone will come to claim them?"

"Nope. But we'll do whatever is fair."

Velvet Wendell sat up with the robe still around her. "What did
you get in return for the horses?"

"News," Brannon stated as he went over to check on Waldo
Vance.

"Did he say news?" Velvet addressed Fletcher.

Fletcher just shrugged.

It took them two hours to rig a stretcher for Abner Cheney, who was now conscious enough to begin to command Trevor and Deputy Giles as they prepared to take him out of the mountains.

"Cheney, you get a doc to put something on that wound to kill that infection and keep those bandages clean and tight," Brannon instructed.

"Brannon, I can't decide whether to thank you for helping us out of that scrape with Vance or have the marshall arrest you for trespassing," Cheney admitted.

"Well," Brannon smiled, "you go get yourself doctored up, and then we'll just fight it out again."

"Mr. Cheney," the marshall said slowly, "listen to me carefully. I'm not coming up in these mountains again unless you have a signed order from a federal judge ordering me to do so. You don't own all of Colorado yet."

Trevor led the party south. Deputy Giles rode one of the stretcher carriers, and Cheney bounced along between the two plodding horses.

Marshall Rosser with Waldo Vance, hands tied behind his back and feet strapped into the stirrups, started out east over the narrow mountain trail.

The marshall turned to Brannon. "Son, I'll buy you a steak supper next time you get to Denver."

"Marshall, if we can get this gold out of the mountain, I'll buy you the whole steer! Are you sure you won't need any help with Vance?"

"Nope," the marshall said with a wink, "if he gives me any trouble, I'll just shoot him."

"Well, don't go up by those boulders behind the mine. I figure there are still a couple bear traps up there," Brannon warned.

By the middle of the afternoon, no one was left at the mine but Brannon, Fletcher, and Wendell. Except for fresh graves dug down by the creek, the scene looked peaceful and quiet. The winds came up from the northwest, and heavy storm clouds began to stack up in Trabajacito Creek canyon.

Brannon and Fletcher spent most of the next morning inside the gold mine making plans. Velvet Wendell, finally regaining her strength, joined them about noon on her first inspection of the mine.

"The way I figure it," Brannon said to Fletcher, ignoring Miss Wendell, "we should bust out good samples of that lode, use a couple of those horses for packing, and take the ore to the assay office. This would give us the basis for a loan to get some men and equipment up here in the spring to start really hauling this stuff out of here."

"You figure we'll crush it up here or haul ore elsewhere?" Wendell asked.

"We'll have to hire someone with equipment to cut a decent road past the falls so we can bring wagons up. That shouldn't be too difficult since that old photographer rolled a wagon right into camp. Then we can start to build some buildings. What do you figure, Edwin, should we start with a dozen men? We'll need a bunkhouse, cook, and a cistern, right?"

"Perhaps Wishy Boswick will send a line into the mine," Fletcher pondered.

"Do either of you know anything about a stamp mill?" Velvet Wendell pushed.

"She's got a point, Stuart," Fletcher prodded him.

"Look," Brannon offered, "if none of Vance's gang double back in the next few days, then one of us will head to town to get some bankers lined up on the deal. Miss Wendell can go back home then."

"Brannon, are you cutting me out of this?" she asked.

"Look, we appreciate your help. I think five hundred dollars should compensate you for your time, but I'm not sure you were ever cut into this," Brannon insisted.

"Now, Brannon, really," Fletcher interrupted. "I assumed that matter was settled out on the hillside."

"Fletcher, don't let years of tea and crumpets soften your logic."

"Come on, Brannon, that's uncalled for. I believe Miss Wendell has a sincere claim on one-fourth—"

"And I think you've sat on silk cushions and drawn your allowance for too many years. As I recall, you didn't lose your cattle ranch in Arizona and come up into these mountains flat broke. You didn't have to watch—"

Velvet Wendell broke in. "No, he didn't watch his wife and baby die in his arms! So what?"

Stuart Brannon raised the back of his hand as though to slap her, but suddenly Fletcher dove at him and knocked him against the cave wall. Brannon came up swinging and caught Fletcher with a right cross in the chin, dropping the Englishman to his knees. He tackled Brannon, banging his head on the wet rock floor of the tunnel. Both men threw punches as they rolled into the darkness of the mine.

"Wait!" Velvet Wendell screamed. "Stop it! You two are acting like you're in some cheap bar in Ft. Worth. Brannon, you're treating me like some crib girl in a Denver back alley, and, Fletcher, you're acting like I'm some helpless lass who needs a grand Cromwellian Protector. Well, let me tell you, I'm neither," she screamed. "I can handle the likes of either of you, separately or together. It wouldn't be the first time nor probably the last. I don't need judgment, and I don't need protection."

"And I say you're going back to town where—"

"Where I belong, Brannon? Listen, buster, I've spent my entire life scraping just to survive. I've served drinks, took in laundry, cooked meals, and mended britches until I can't count the houses, towns, or counties where I've lived."

"The point is—" Brannon started.

"Let her finish," Fletcher insisted.

"Look, I've broken my back for years. That's why I look forty instead of thirty-two. But finally something nice happens. A wounded old man with a big heart staggers into my life. For a few weeks someone needs me. And for a few weeks, I felt like I was doing something important.

"Everett Davis was kind enough to open a door so I could get out of that rut I called life. Well, listen, Mister, not you, not that Englishman, nobody is going to cut me out of my share. You might hang me, or shoot me, or feed me to the bears, but I'm staying, so quit acting like a couple of schoolboys and face up to the fact that you're stuck with me as a full partner!"

Her final words echoed up and down the tunnel.

"I say, that was—" Fletcher began.

"And don't give me any of that condescending 'well-said' garbage!" she snapped.

Brannon glanced over at Fletcher, paused, and then nodded.

"Did she pass?" Fletcher asked.

"No doubts in my mind." Brannon smiled. "And you, Edwin?"

"My word, can you fault a lady who invokes Cromwell?"

"Wait a minute," she yelled. "Wait a minute . . . do you mean that you put on a sham just to make me angry?"

"There are standers and there are runners," Brannon replied. "We had to find out if you were a stander. It won't be easy to develop and hold on to this mine."

"And I passed?" she asked softly.

"With flying colors!" Fletcher beamed.

"You're quite a scrappy lady," Brannon admitted.

"And you two are thoughtless derelicts," she returned. "If you ever, ever try something like this again, I will personally claw your eyes out of your insensitive melonheads!"

Fletcher glanced down at his feet and then up at Brannon. "I say, I believe she means it."

"Well, at least we understand each other." Brannon broke into a smile and walked out of the mine.

EIGHT

It never sprinkles in the upper reaches of the Trabajacito canyon.
It never rains lightly.
Not even a mild storm.

It is clear. Or it pours down. Or it snows.

That's all.

At least, that's how Stuart Brannon had it figured.

For three full days the rains had drenched the dusty, dry mountainside. The creek now ran full, and it was dangerous to try to cross it. The log barrier hastily erected to provide protection from gunfire now served as a backstop for a mud slide. The small yard and campfire sported a pond from six to twelve inches deep. The dugout cabin leaked bucketsful of mud, sticks, and rocks as the roof melted and the logs began to shift. The only absolutely dry spot was in the short tunnel from the cabin fireplace to the mine and just inside the mine entrance itself.

For days Brannon and Fletcher had been digging at the main strata of the lode, trying to get enough gold-embedded quartz to impress the bankers and pay for winter's supplies. Stripped to the waist, they dug, picked, chipped, hammered, drilled, clawed, carried, and blasted away for twelve to fourteen hours a day.

Velvet Wendell tried to keep water, coffee, and hot meals coming to the men. But when the cabin finally collapsed, she too moved into the mine and began wheeling out as much ore as she could push. Neither man tried to stop her from doing the heavy work.

On the third night, the rain stopped at sunset, and the clouds blew away quickly. The temperature dropped dramatically. Brannon and Fletcher scurried around in the twilight scrounging up any wood dry enough to burn. They built a huge bonfire near the entrance to the mine and huddled close to keep warm.

Brannon had taken three canvas pack tarps and cut holes in the centers, forming crude ponchos for each of them. All three had become so drenched and dirty that it had become hard to distinguish one person from another at a distance. In fact, as Brannon kidded them, it was getting difficult to tell them from the mud itself.

"I say," Fletcher began, "I don't believe I've been this cold since Trudeaux and I stumbled into the cabin at Broken Arrow Crossing."

"Yeah, it gives a guy a sinking feeling to think of going through another winter like that," Brannon added.

"Are we going to live in this mine shaft all winter?" Velvet gasped.

"We'd be a pack of raving lunatics by spring." Fletcher laughed.

"Well," Brannon began, "I've got one plan. I suggest that you two head to Denver with three packloads of our best ore."

"Denver?" Fletcher questioned.

"Yep. That's the only place that will have enough supplies, men, mining engineers, and bankers to get this type of operation started up." Brannon rubbed his hands over the fire. "Your job, Fletcher, is to make the financial contacts and hire an engineer."

"And what's my job?" Velvet asked.

"First, buy yourself a new dress and a hat. That's the ugliest, dirtiest dress I've ever seen. Right, Fletcher?"

"What? You expect me to enter your battle?"

"The dress, Edwin, eh . . . how would you describe the dress under that muddy poncho?"

"Well, actually, Miss Wendell, it is rather horrid."

"But that's not all!" Brannon went on. "Velvet, you will need to buy us office space in a building and establish an office. You will need to stay in Denver during the winter and run that office, seeing that all the paperwork gets done, the accounts paid, and supplies secured and stored until we can transport them out to the mine. Can you do that?"

"I think I can handle it," she answered.

"So do I," Brannon affirmed.

"And you, Brannon?" Fletcher pressed.

"For now, I'll stick it out up here. We have too many visitors to leave her vacant, no matter how much paper we hold. I'll try to pull together a winter-tight cabin and guard the claim."

"A cabin? By yourself?" Velvet probed.

"Well, for a pot of beans and some sourdough, I think I can hire a couple Utes to help me wrestle the logs. Then, Fletcher, you'll need to make one trip up here before winter with more supplies and spell me. I've got to ride out and track down Everett's killer. Then I'll climb back up here and let Edwin spend the winter in Denver sweet-talking the bankers."

"Sounds like you'll have a long, lonely winter," she observed.

"Yep. Some folks do better in cities, and some winter better like bears in the woods. As you've discovered, my sparkling personality fits the wilderness better than State Street."

"Mr. Brannon, I don't think—"

"Stuart. I'm Mr. Brannon to employees, but to partners I'm Stuart or Brannon. Not Mister."

"Stuart," she continued, "I don't think I've seen you smile more than ten seconds since we've met. Why is that?"

"That's a good question, Brannon." Fletcher stood to warm himself. "If you aren't worried or fuming, you're plotting, planning, or fighting."

Velvet Wendell pushed her soaked hat off her head, letting it dangle by the stampede string. She scratched her muddy forehead with the back of her hand and took a sip of coffee. "What do you do for fun, anyway?"

"Well, now, this is a reassuring situation!" Brannon complained. "I'm sending my partners to town to do serious business, and they're thinking only of parties!"

Fletcher turned to Velvet. "Actually, Brannon's idea of a grand time is to window-shop at the feed store."

"Why, I bet he's the type who asks a girl out to attend the fat sale at the stockyard," she ribbed.

"Brannon, didn't you tell me that the only holiday you ever took was to go to Chicago and buy a bull?"

"You do dance, don't you?" she asked.

"Not since that hot horseshoe slipped down his boot!" Fletcher responded.

"All right! I see that you two are enjoying yourself at my expense."

"We could go on . . . " Fletcher offered.

"Look, I'm glad you two are having fun, but we need to make some plans. There's no reason not to send you off tomorrow if the weather permits."

"Excuse me, sir, but I just put in fourteen hours in a gold mine, and it is time to dance." Fletcher turned and bowed to Velvet Wendell. "I beg your pardon, Miss, but do you have any openings on your dance card this evening?"

Velvet Wendell stood and curtseyed. "Why, thank you for asking, sir. I am rather committed, but I do have one slot left for the next dance."

"Would you accept my invitation, or are you with this gentleman?"

"Him? Oh, heavens! He's my . . . my father!"

"Father!" Brannon moaned.

"Well, old-timer," Fletcher joshed, "you certainly have a lovely daughter."

Brannon just stared.

"Don't mind him," Velvet added. "He's a tad deaf, blind, and humorless." She stood and accepted Fletcher's outstretched hand. "Oh, my, what is this number the band's playing?"

"I believe it's a Strauss waltz, isn't it?" Fletcher suggested.

"Yes, of course . . . you're right." She nodded.

For the next several minutes, while Fletcher hummed "Tales from the Vienna Woods," he and Velvet stumbled and danced their way around the campfire.

Finally, they plopped down next to Brannon, still laughing and humming.

"Well, sir," Fletcher shouted in Brannon's ear, "thank you so much for allowing me the honor of dancing with your delightful daughter."

"That was the worst dancing I have ever seen in my life," Brannon replied.

"Why, thank you," Fletcher said with a smile.

She giggled. "My father is a noted expert in the field of social dancing."

"And if you ever lay hands on my daughter again, I'll slice you up in tiny pieces and feed you to the javelinas."

"Finally," Velvet shouted with laughter, "he's starting to loosen up."

"Not really," Fletcher objected. "I believe he was quite serious about that."

"You know what you are, Stuart Brannon?" Velvet Wendell chimed in. "You are everyone's older brother! Oh, you might be a young man, but you act like it's your calling to keep everyone on earth on the narrow path. If the Lord had a couple more like you, He could retire."

"I think maybe this is going too far," Brannon mumbled.

"Oh, don't take it wrong," she said soothingly. "It feels sort of nice to have an older brother. I predict that when Stuart Brannon dies, which will be at a very old age, it will be one of the largest funerals ever held in the state. Every 'little' brother and 'little' sister will be there. But no one will stand around the grave saying, 'Remember all those good times we had?'"

"Quite right," Fletcher continued. "They will just say, 'Do you remember the time he jumped in and bailed me out?'"

"Yes!" She raised her voice and waved her arms as she said, "They'll tell of how he built their barn when it burned to the ground, or hauled their kids a hundred miles through the snow to the doctors, or captured the gang that was stealing their cows, or wrestled a mountain lion just to save their little Blue Heeler."

"If you two have had enough . . . I feel like a slab of venison slowly turning over the fire."

"You're right, of course," Miss Wendell reflected. "Thank you for allowing us to relax at your expense. It's the first time in ages that I haven't been cramped up with worry."

Brannon looked at her eyes. Even in the firelight a sparkle that he had never noticed radiated there.

Quite a lady in her prime. Lord, she's still in her prime! Maybe You could sort of lighten her load a little? I'll take the slack. Give her enough good times to be a delight to her memory.

He grabbed up a lantern and walked back into the tunnel and then returned carrying a black ledger and a very short stub of a pencil.

"Look, like it or not, we will need to do a little business. Miss Wendell—"

"My friends call me Vel."

"What do your partners call you?"

"I don't know, I've never had any before."

"Well, Miss Vel . . . please don't take this personal, but can you read and write?"

"Of course, you didn't think—"

"Vel, I sincerely didn't want to assume anything and embarrass you. Lots of folks out here never had an opportunity to attend school. But when I heard you mention Cromwell, I figured you spent some time with the books."

"Why do you ask?"

"We've got to do some figurin'. And since you'll be running the office in Denver, you'll need to know certain things. It might be best if you mark this down in your own writing so you can read it when you're done."

He handed the pencil and ledger to her.

For the next two hours as the stars got brighter and the temperature colder, they huddled at the fire and charted the course of action for the next several months.

Finally it was Fletcher who interrupted Brannon.

"Stuart, either you're getting real slurred in speech or I'm falling asleep." He stood up and stretched.

"You're right. That's enough planning. If we can't get the initial financing, we wasted our time anyway. Let's call it a day, *compadres*."

"Stuart, can I talk with you a moment?" Velvet stood and walked around the fire to where he was leaning against a boulder.

"I gave you quite a bit of work to do when you get to Denver, didn't I?" Brannon admitted.

"Yes, you did," she agreed. "But . . . well, look, I don't want to sound melodramatic, but you and Edwin . . . "

Brannon could see the trace of tears plowing down her face.

"Are you all right?" he asked.

"Stuart, today you and Edwin treated me like an equal partner. I've never been treated that way by men—or by women. It feels good, real good."

Brannon cleared his throat. "Yeah, well, once in a while I do things right. Maybe that can begin to make up for a little suspicion and greed earlier."

"You know," she continued, "I don't know how old you are, but you'll always be my older brother. Thanks, Stuart, it's nice to be part of a family after all these years."

She turned quickly and retreated into the mine tunnel carrying one of the two kerosene lanterns.

"I say, Brannon," Fletcher called as he was stirring the fire, "I say, where are you going?"

"I'll check the horses," Brannon managed to mumble.

The horses, as Brannon and Fletcher both knew, were just fine.

He hunkered down in his poncho alongside the creek and began tossing pebbles into the swollen stream. The soft starlight reflected off the splashing water, and the night breeze slowed to a mere whisper. His hands and face were cold, but his mind was racing.

Lord, I came up here to make a stake and get back to my ranch in Arizona. But the more complications, the tougher it's going to be to leave. Today's probably the first decent day I've had in six months, too. This isn't my place, Lord. I don't belong up in these mountains. I don't know if I want to own a gold mine. Help me find a way to go home soon.

"You busy?"

Brannon jumped to his feet with one hand on the grip of his pistol.

"Oh . . . Vel! Listen, no, yes. Just talking to the Lord, I guess."
Even in the moonlight, he could see her sudden confusion.

"Yes . . . actually, I mean—" she stammered.

"Hey, it's all right." He started walking back toward the mine.
"Things get out of whack sometimes, and I've just got to get my
head clear. What can I do for you?"

"Actually, it was nothing important. I wondered if I could take
this buffalo robe with me? It will come in handy on the trip out,
and it sort of reminds me of Mr. Davis."

"That's a good idea. Listen, when you get that office established
in Denver, tack that on the wall, and it will remind us all of
Everett."

It was a good night.
No pain.
No dreams.
No interruptions.

Brannon woke to frost on his blanket and daylight already
reflecting off the tops of the highest mountains. Neither of the
other two was up yet. By instinct, he turned his boots upside down
and banged them against a rock before pulling them on. His mind
had wandered back to his ranch in Arizona, but his body shuffled
around the muddy campsite. Soon a small fire snapped and crack-
led, and flashes of heat began to warm Brannon and the coffeepot
that hung from an iron bar stretched over the flames.

He poured out a fresh basin of water and then scouted around
in what was left of the cabin. In a matter of moments he had
propped up a broken piece of mirror and was busy shaving off his
stubby beard. Brannon stared at the bronze creases stretching
away from his eyes.

There he is, folks—everybody's older brother!

He ambled back to the cabin and emerged with a square chunk
of lard soap and a comb. Brannon pulled off the deerskin shirt and
shivered as the frigid morning air clutched his bare chest. The
water in the basin was even colder, but he splashed himself and
scrubbed away at the dust and dirt.

Two basins of water later, Brannon glanced into the little mirror fragment and parted his hair. Then he turned to the fire and fluffed it up. He poured boiling coffee into a tin cup. Sitting down on a fairly dry log, he glanced up at the clear morning sky. Down the canyon he could see that the aspen, which only recently had turned color, were now beginning to drop leaves.

The next storm will be snow. Colorado winter! It will be a long time before we walk on dry ground again.

"My, oh my! Would you look at that! You could break the heart of every girl in Virginia City."

Brannon looked up and saw Velvet Wendell grinning at his clean-shaven face.

"Well, even elder brothers clean up once in a while," he confessed.

"I'm sorry I went on about that," she apologized.

"Hey, don't worry about it. I'm so dumb I thought it was a compliment."

"You haven't made plans to go to town yourself, have you?" she teased.

"No, it's just, well, it seems like I've spent the past several weeks just reacting to one disaster after another. So now it's time to get things back under my control. Cleanin' up seemed to be a good place to begin."

Velvet picked up the little piece of mirror and looked at herself.

"You know what, Mr. Brannon? I'm looking more and more like my mother. Only dirtier. A hot bath and a new dress will change my whole outlook on life."

She poured herself a cup of coffee and sat down next to him. "You don't know very much about me, do you?" she asked.

"Nope . . . I don't guess I do."

"Would you like to know about me?"

"Only the part you want to tell."

"I don't want to tell you any of it."

"That's fair enough."

"Aren't you curious?"

"Vel . . . I like you just as you are right now. It's really not necessary for me to know any more about your past."

She sat and sipped her coffee.

Finishing the cup, she looked at Brannon. "Well, big brother, what are you going to do today?"

"After I get you two kids sent off to school, I need to teach that horse to drive so I can pull some logs in here for a decent cabin."

"How about your Indian help? Where will you find your Ute friends?"

"Oh, they'll come wandering into camp about ten minutes after you and Fletcher leave."

"You mean they're watching us even now?"

"Probably."

"That's rather an uncomfortable feeling," she confessed.

"Why? Are you planning on doing something embarrassing?"

"Of course not!"

"Then just smile and wave."

"Wave? Where are they?" she asked.

"Over there." He pointed to the distant mountain slope.

Velvet Wendell smiled and waved at the bleak mountain.

"Or maybe this time they're over near the back of that mountain," he continued.

Quickly, Velvet turned and offered a wave to the big mountain to the east.

"Or," Brannon added, "perhaps they're just down in the cottonwoods next to the creek."

"Stuart Brannon, you're making sport of me!" She feigned a pout.

"Hey, you have a nice wave," he joked. "You ought to be a politician's wife."

"You know," she said laughing, "the back of my hand works very nicely, too."

"I'm sure it does, but I already said I didn't need to hear about your past."

"You know, Mr. Brannon, I am either going to miss you very much, or I won't bother thinking about you at all. I just can't decide which."

"Thank you," he said, standing up and refilling his coffee cup.

It took two more hours to get the horse string packed with ore samples and send Fletcher and Wendell off down the mountain. They agreed that the best route for such a load would be to go straight to Tres Casas and attempt to buy a wagon. From there, they could cut across the mountains near El Rio de las Ánimas Perdidas and turn north along the eastern slope until they reached Denver.

It was shorter to cut across the mountains on the trail that the marshall had followed. But the feel of snow made that trip increasingly dangerous. If all went well, Brannon hoped that Fletcher could make it back in a month with supplies for the winter.

After they left, Brannon spent the next couple of hours hiking among the better stands of trees, marking ones to cut for a cabin. He knew it would be a race against time.

It will be simple and stout. A good fireplace and gun slits. In the spring, we'll bring up a circular saw and put up some decent buildings—bunk house, cook shack, supply building, derrick on the shaft.

All morning he expected company. Red Shirt and his friends were due to report in.

"Of course," Brannon mumbled to himself, "maybe they did ride off to the canyons!"

After a lunch of half a loaf of bread and a can of tomatoes, he set out to cut trees. It was late in the day before he had three trees down, bucked, and cut to length. He let them lay for the night. Carrying a crosscut saw and his Winchester over his shoulder, he headed back to the mine.

When he puffed his way into the clearing, Red Shirt was sitting in front of a bright-burning fire drinking coffee.

Brannon nodded to the Indian as he put down the saw and leaned the rifle against the log barrier. "Help yourself to the coffee," he told Red Shirt.

"No, thank you." Red Shirt smiled and kept drinking from the tin cup.

"I thought you might come down and help me cut those trees."

"If you want to work like a beaver, that's your decision. I

decided to rest like an otter," Red Shirt announced. "I believe it's time to eat."

"Where are your brothers?" Brannon asked.

"They are in the mountains still. Perhaps they stopped to hunt."

"Were you with them?"

"No, I followed the limping man, the wounded one, and the young lawman."

"What happened to them?"

"Nothing. Was something supposed to happen?"

"No, I mean, where did they end up?"

"I have no idea." Red Shirt shrugged.

"But you followed them!"

"I followed them for three days. That was all that the Brannon asked. They did not end their journey, but continued traveling down the trail past the hot springs."

"Yeah, good. Now, how about the marshall—you know, the older lawman?"

"Crazy Waters and Chalco—they followed him. Where are the beans?"

Brannon dug the iron Dutch oven out of the coals and brushed embers from the lid. He pried out a new loaf of sourdough bread and then motioned towards an iron pot hanging beside the coffee. "The beans are there. But you'll have to shovel out your own grub. This isn't a cantina."

It was almost dark when Crazy Waters and Chalco returned. They carried a small deer across the front of the sorrel. Flopping the meat down near the fire, they immediately turned to Red Shirt and began an excited and agitated conversation.

Stuart Brannon could only watch and wait.

Finally, Red Shirt turned to him and blurted out, "It is bad, very bad."

"What happened?"

"The old lawman is dead."

"The marshall? How? What happened?"

"They followed for two days, and all was peaceful. But on the third day three men hidden in the trees shoot the old lawman.

Then they untie the little man, and he shoots the lawman some more. Then they ride away."

"Who were the men?"

"Your visitors."

"Vance's men? Some that were here at the camp?"

"Yes, some of those men."

Brannon banged his clenched right fist into the palm of his left hand.

"You should have killed them all. An enemy who escapes death will come back twice as strong," said Red Shirt. He motioned for the others to help themselves to the food.

Brannon started to walk down to the creek.

"The Brannon is not hungry?" Red Shirt called.

He didn't bother replying but kept going until he reached the banks of the now-decreasing Trabajacito.

Lord, what's going on here?

Every disaster leads to another one!

I'm stuck guarding the gold again.

It's not right. It's just not right. I fumed here for a month wanting to find out who gunned down Everett Davis. Now the marshall is dead, and I know who did it.

Brannon paced back and forth along the banks of the stream. By instinct he pulled his pistol, cracked it open, inspected the chamber, and then closed it.

There was no question what he had to do.

Lord, some things in life are more important than all the gold in Colorado and all the cattle in Arizona! This country won't be worth a Confederate dollar if there isn't any justice.

Immediately he began to hike back to the fire.

Lord, help me.

"The Brannon will eat now?" Red Shirt looked up from his plate.

"Yep. Red Shirt, I want to trade again. Are you ready?"

"More news?"

"Nope. No more news. I want you, Crazy Waters, and Chalco to stay here in camp and guard this mine for me."

"The Brannon is leaving?"

"Yep."

"You going after the killers?"

"Yep."

"I thought so."

"I'll need you to camp right here and don't let anyone come across the river to the mine."

"For how long do we camp here?"

"One month—a new moon, do you understand?"

"I understand. September has thirty days and October thirty-one," Red Shirt said proudly.

"Where did you learn that?"

"Kansas."

Brannon looked at Red Shirt. "When were you in Kansas?"

"I went to school there for a while. Then they dismissed me."

"Why?"

"I was too smart. After school there was nothing to do, so I raced horses."

"What's wrong with that?" Brannon asked.

"I won all the races," Red Shirt said smiling. "If we guard your hole in the ground for thirty-one days, what will you give us?"

"All the supplies that are here."

"Everything?"

"Yes, if I do not come back in thirty-one days, you can haul off whatever you want."

"And if you do come back?"

"I will bring you a present."

"What kind of present?"

"Rifles, blankets, candy—things like that."

"And canned tomatoes?" Red Shirt asked.

"Yep."

"Maybe we will carry off everything tomorrow and go and live in the canyons," Red Shirt said without emotion.

"Maybe you will," Brannon said shrugging, "maybe you will."

NINE

Stuart Brannon set the saddle down lightly. Operating from habit, he walked around to the off side and drew the stirrup from the horn, allowing the cinch to fall down towards the muddy Colorado clay. Returning to the near side, he tugged at the Navajo blanket near the fork, and then threw his weight into the *latigo*. The roan horse pranced at the tight cinch.

The clouds again hung heavy, and the air was thick with the feel of rain. *It's probably snowing up there,* he thought as he glanced at distant peaks in the San Juans. Slipping the headstall over the horse's ears, he adjusted the bit and let the reins drop straight down.

Then he walked back to what was left of the dugout cabin and hauled out the gear he had rounded up. A skillet, a grub sack, two blankets, his worn-out coat, Lisa's picture, and Everett Davis's Bible. He rolled them tightly in a scrap of oil cloth and tied them to the back of the cantle.

Brannon returned to the fire where Red Shirt, Crazy Waters, and Chalco crouched by the flames. He sat down on a boulder and pulled his knife. Routinely, he began scraping the mud off his boots. He noticed that the soles were thin, and the leather around the welt was extremely cracked.

"The Brannon is leaving now? It will rain soon," Red Shirt commented.

"Yep, I'm heading out. Remember our deal?"

"We will stay and eat your food for a month. Then we will carry off all we can. We will go to lower ground."

"Unless I return before you leave!" Brannon insisted.

Crazy Waters spoke, and then Red Shirt turned to Brannon.

"He said, 'Good-bye, the Brannon, we will not see you again.'"

"Tell him, if he leaves before the month is out, he will see me behind every tree, and beside every cholla, and in the midst of every dream."

Red Shirt repeated the words to an apprehensive Crazy Waters. Then he turned back to Brannon. "Round Hat is evil. He will try to shoot you in the back."

"Yes," Brannon added, "I believe you are right. But I will come back here."

"How do you know?"

"Faith."

"Faith? You mean, like faith in the Jesus God?"

"Yep. That's a big part of it." Brannon walked towards the waiting horse, and the Indians walked with him. "And it's a faith that God rewards you for doing what's right." He jerked the cinch tighter and reset the *latigo*. Then he pulled the reins up over the horse's head and with his left hand grabbed a handful of the roan's mane. Grabbing the saddle horn with his right hand, he jammed his left foot into the stirrup and gently swung his right leg over the horse.

It was not Sage.

But the saddle was the same, and it felt very comfortable to be horseback again.

"Red Shirt, don't eat too much and get sick," he said laughing.

Crazy Waters shouted a parting, but Brannon had no idea what he said. It could have been a curse or a blessing. It didn't matter. He was soon out of sight.

For the first time in months, Stuart Brannon felt truly free.

Crazy Waters and Chalco had told Red Shirt that the old lawman had been bushwhacked on the last meadow of the eastern slope of the mountains before they hit the plains. Brannon hoped it was on the main eastern trail. Otherwise he would have to check out about ten thousand different meadows.

The marshall would have been in no hurry to blaze new trails. He must have taken the most-used and direct route through. Vance, on the other hand—he'd have to go to town and buy more men. Two or three hired guns would never satisfy him. He'll be somewhere between the meadow and Denver.

It started raining about noon. With the wind at his back, Brannon didn't notice how severe the storm was until he realized that his coat was soaked. Because of earlier storms, it didn't take long for the trail to slick up, dashing all hopes of following hoof-prints.

Roany slowed his pace in the muddy afternoon, and Brannon, chilled to the bone, started looking for shelter. Holding out for a cabin or shack of some kind, he crossed one ridge of trees after another. Reaching timberline about dark, he considered riding back into the forest when he sighted a cave right at the edge of the timber. He approached the opening cautiously, not knowing what kind of beast, human or animal, he might encounter.

A small circle of wet ashes at the shallow granite entrance and packed dirt at the back signaled that it had most recently hosted human habitants. Two log rounds, seemingly used for benches, were at the back of the cave.

He pulled the saddle and gear off the horse and jammed his belongings into the cave. Brannon led the horse down to a grove of fir trees and picketed him where he would get some protection from the wind and storm. Breaking off dead wood at the bottom of trees, he soon had an armful of half-dry firewood.

With some effort, he finally got the fire going. It was just enough under the overhang of the cave to protect it from some of the storm, yet not so much that the cave would smoke out. He used one of the rounds for a stool and tossed the other on the fire. He was too wet to worry about cooking supper and just chewed on a piece of jerky and a leftover biscuit that had miraculously stayed dry.

He pulled off his wet jacket and stuck it on a pole near the fire. Then he tossed the second "stool" on the fire, wrapped himself in the two blankets, and lay down in a dry spot, resting his head on his saddle.

Brannon had a fitful night's sleep. He was cold and wet, and he kept dreaming about being in a sandstorm with sand continuously stinging his face. It was way before daylight, with the embers of the fire still glowing, when it dawned on him that the stinging sensation had nothing to do with dreams.

"Fleas!" he shouted.

As he staggered towards the fire, he could feel them all over his body. Banging out his boots, he yanked them on and hurried to toss some more wood on the fire. Soon it blazed in the heavy, cold, clear Colorado night.

He still couldn't see the insects, but he waved his hands through the flames and hurriedly rubbed the pests from his arms. He stripped off his shirt and pants, giving them the fire treatment as well. Pulling on his coat that had dried out safe from the fleas, he propped his other clothing as close to the fire as possible to kill the pests and yet not catch the clothing on fire.

Brannon spent the next two hours before daylight trying to stay warm and attempting to pick fleas out of his hair. He was tired, sore, and still itching when he remounted Roany and headed out. The heavy clouds began to break up by noon, and as he crossed the granite mountain pass, he could still see signs of snow that had fallen the previous night. Once he started down the eastern slope of the mountains, the winds picked up behind him. Soon the sky was clear and very cold. Roany plodded away, one step after another, needing an occasional spur in the flank to hasten the pace.

The sun had not set when Brannon noticed that ice was beginning to form on the outside edges of the mud puddles.

"Well, at least it will freeze these biting varmits crawling all over me!" he muttered to Roany.

He came across the top end of a meadow and realized that he had no idea if this was the last one before the plains or not. Finding a battered cabin on the north side of the meadow, he decided to call it a day. The whole west end of the cabin had collapsed, but the east end still sported a fairly complete fireplace, and the timbers and floor were dry. Firewood was abundant, and

Brannon discovered several outbuildings in a dilapidated condition.

After a hot supper of the saltiest fried meat he had ever tasted and a cup of coffee boiled in his tin cup, Brannon lay down by the fire and fell asleep.

A dim gray daylight filtered through the unchinked logs to let Brannon know that he had overslept. Every muscle in his body ached. He staggered to his feet and found he was so stove-up he could barely walk. His feet and hands were almost numb from cold.

"Well, it isn't raining—and the fleas froze! Lord, I don't want to sound ungrateful, but I'd give about half that gold mine for a hot bath, new clothes, and a bed with clean linen sheets."

Brannon remembered some of the long days on the trail, waking up cold and wet and seeing the old-timers barely able to roll out. "I'm too old for the trail," they would moan.

Now it was his turn. Still a few weeks shy of being thirty, Brannon felt "too old for the trail."

When he reached the far end of the meadow, he could see another meadow lower down the mountain, so he spurred the roan gelding, and they slipped their way down the icy trail. Most of the morning was spent dropping down out of the mountains from one meadow to another. The weather warmed slightly as he descended. The ice gave way to slush and then to mud.

Finally he climbed over a partially wooded pass and could see the great plains stretching out for hundreds of miles to the east. Right in front of him was a meadow with the grass already frozen brown. He circled the meadow looking for signs of the ambush.

The tedious search revealed nothing at all.

No tracks.

No body.

No campfires.

Brannon circled the meadow again, this time about fifty feet outside the circumference of the meadow. Once again, there were no clues.

"Well, Roany, one more time around Jericho. If the walls don't fall down this time, we've got to find a new meadow."

At the bottom end of the wide circle, where the sagebrush lapped into the squatty cedars and pinon pines, Brannon noticed a few broken limbs of sage. Projecting a line from the meadow to the bush, he rode on a northeast course, following occasionally broken sage until he spotted a granite outcropping. The jagged rocks and boulders shoved out of the surrounding ground like a giant angry fist just breaking through the earth's surface.

The pounding rain and accompanying runoff of the previous days had erased any markings that might have existed. After one trip horseback around the rocks, he dismounted and tied Roany to a sage. Then he set out to climb the rocky mound. The top of the rocks revealed nothing more than a slightly better view of the surrounding plains.

Coming down off the rocks in the opposite direction, Brannon's boot heel caught on a boulder, and he began to tumble backwards. He jammed his hand into the rocks to catch himself and scraped the knuckles on his left hand raw as they wedged down between some smaller rocks.

He pulled his scraped hand up quickly and examined his wounds. Without thinking much about it, Brannon pulled off his bandana and tied it around his bleeding knuckles. He peered down at the hole his hand had punched into the gravel.

"What?" he blurted out.

Dropping to his knees, he frantically began to pull away the rough boulders and rocks with his hands.

"It's a boot!" he stammered.

Stuart Brannon knew what he would find under the rocks.

Both hands were sore and raw by the time he was able to pull the marshall's lifeless body out of the rocky grave.

He stood up and took several deep breaths of fresh cold air. Then he turned the body over. The cold and the shallow burial had delayed decay, and Brannon could see the marshall's wounds.

Shot by a rifle, twice in the lower back, he decided. *And then . . .*

Brannon turned away from the body and sat down.

At that moment he couldn't tell whether it was anger, rage, shock, or nausea. He was losing control, control of his feelings, his emotions, his breakfast.

He rested his chest against his legs and dropped his head between his knees. Regaining his strength, he rolled the marshall over on his back.

He had seen enough.

Marshall Rosser had been repeatedly shot in the back of the head at close range after receiving the other wounds, and probably after he was dead.

"You'll hang for this one, Vance!" he vowed. He struggled to carry the marshall's body on down off the rocks.

Brannon spent the best part of the afternoon scraping out a grave with his frying pan among the sagebrush on the edge of the prairie. Wrapping the marshall in one of his blankets, he covered the lawman and tamped down the dirt. There was nothing to use to mark the grave.

He pulled Everett Davis's tattered Bible from his grub bag and squatted next to the freshly turned and slightly muddy grave.

After reading a little from Psalms and Revelation, Brannon stood.

"Lord, I didn't know him. I don't know what he did good or bad. I have no idea what he thought of You. Just make sure the books read that he died trying to make this wild country tame. He didn't get paid enough or thanked enough for this."

Brannon rolled up the marshall's hat and badge with his gear on the back of the saddle and remounted. The sweat on his body from all the digging was turning icy cold as he left the grave and trotted lower down the mountain slope toward what looked like a wagon rut heading north and south.

Reaching the primitive road, he turned north.

Somewhere up ahead was Denver.

And Waldo Vance.

Stuart Brannon's right hand gripped the rifle stock, his finger feather-light against the trigger, and his thumb on the hammer.

The Winchester bounced across his lap and occasionally banged into the fork of the saddle. His grip tightened as he saw two men approaching, heading south on the trail. He stopped, waiting for them to ride alongside.

First one, then the other dismounted. Brannon did the same.

"Evenin', men."

"Evenin'," the taller one replied.

"You headed into Conchita?" the shorter one asked, looking over Brannon's rifle that he still held in his hand.

He nodded. "How much further up the trail?"

"Maybe an hour," the man replied. Pulling out some makings, he began to roll a quirly.

Both Brannon and the taller man declined the man's offer to share supplies.

"Well, we'd better get going. Don't know how long it is until we hit the next town," the taller one added.

As the men remounted, the shorter man with the dirty gray hat turned to Brannon. "Say, did you come up from the south?"

"Nope. From the west."

"Down from the mountains?"

"Yep."

"Well, you don't happen to know how far it is to Kinsalvy?"

"Kinsalvy? No, I haven't heard of that one, but I don't know my way around these parts." Brannon nodded. "But sounds like the kind of place I'd remember—Kinsalvy?"

"Or somethin' like it. We came across a Mexican on the trail and asked him what was the next town we'd hit."

"Yeah, and he told us it was Kinsalvy," the tall man interjected. "He weren't lying now, was he?"

"Kinsalvy . . . are you sure it wasn't *quién sabe?*"

"Yeah, that's it! You been there?"

"Well, gents, that's Spanish for 'who knows?'"

"You mean he didn't know what the next town is?"

"Yep, that's about it."

"Why, I'll be . . . why didn't he just say so?" the tall man exclaimed. "We could have been on the trail all night!"

"Say, you men didn't happen to run across a man named Vance

riding up this trail, did you? A short man with dark brown suit and brown bowler?"

"Not on the trail, but we did run across a fella like that at Mama Grande's."

"He offered us a job. Dollar a day plus expenses to be deputies down in the gold mines."

"Yep, and we turned him down. If there's so much gold you got to hire men to protect it, we figure we'll find a little of it for ourselves."

"Only trouble is, we don't know where it was he came from, except it's somewhere towards New Mexico."

"Well, thanks. Did you say Mama Grande's?"

"Yep. It's sorta like a store, cafe, hotel, and saloon all rolled into one."

"And Mama Grande—she's sorta like four women rolled into one!" the other man said laughing.

As the men rode off, Brannon heard the short one murmur, "Kinsalvy. I still think it's a town, no matter what that old boy says!"

He could be right, Brannon thought. *There've been stranger names.*

Approaching Conchita about sunset, Brannon discovered that the town consisted of a small square dirt plaza from which sprouted an east-leaning flagpole with a tattered U.S. flag and four rows of adobe buildings, each facing the flagpole. It reminded Brannon of a fort without walls or gates.

Spotting a corral on the north side of town, he rode down the dusty road past one group of buildings facing east that seemed to be private residences.

A Mexican boy of about twelve greeted him at the corrals.

"Mister, good hay and water for your *caballo*, only fifty *centavos*."

"Sounds like a deal, son." Brannon dismounted and pulled his gear off the back of the saddle. He jammed his hand into the only pocket in his trousers that wasn't ripped, pulled out a dollar coin, and tossed it to the boy.

"*Dos noches?*"

"Ah, *quizas*. Listen, son, do you have a sheriff here in Conchita?"

The boy stared and tilted his head.

"You know—a sheriff, a marshall?"

"Good hay and water for your *caballo*," the boy offered.

"*¿Donde esta su . . . eh, policia?*" Brannon queried.

"*¿Policia? ¿En Conchita?*" the boy asked laughing.

"How about a mayor? Do you have a . . . an *Alcalde?*"

"Ai! *Si*. Mama Grande!" the boy replied.

"*¿Esta el Alcalde en el cafe Mama Grande?*" Brannon asked.

"No! No!" The boy laughed. "*Mama Grande es la Alcalde!*"

"She's the mayor?" Brannon smiled with the boy. "*Gracias, amigo.*"

"*Hasta la vista, vaquero agotado.*"

Tired cowboy? I'm not exactly a threatening presence.

Mama Grande's had at least five front doors off the covered sidewalk that faced the plaza. On the outside it looked like several different shops, but once inside, Brannon noticed it was one large room divided by shelves, blankets, and merchandise.

It was into the mercantile end of the store that Brannon had stepped. He was greeted by a man in a worn long-sleeved white shirt buttoned at the neck, struggling to carry a small keg of nails. His right wrist was bandaged, and he had bruises on the side of his face.

"Let me give you a hand." Brannon gripped the barrel under his left arm and continued to carry his rifle and bedroll with his right hand. Carrying the nails to the back of the room, he set them down where the man motioned.

"Thanks a bunch, Mister . . . eh . . . "

"Brannon."

"Call me Henry. I got a little banged up yesterday and am laid up a bit. Say, you aren't lookin' for work, are ya? We could use a man who can carry a keg of nails with one arm."

"No, but thanks."

"Listen, the bar's at the other end, and I'd offer to buy you a drink, but . . . come here." He motioned for Brannon to bend down so he could talk softly.

"To tell you the truth," he whispered, "I've seen them mix that poison, and I wouldn't touch that stuff if I were buried up to my neck in a 'Pache anthill, *sabe?*"

"Thanks for the warning." Brannon smiled. "I'll avoid it at all costs. Listen, you don't have a marshall here, do you?"

"No, sir, no lawman for thirty miles. Now every once in a while Marshall Rosser or Deputy Giles comes riding through. Most of the time Mama Grande settles the arguments."

"Thanks. Can I leave this gear back against the wall?"

"Sure. Hey, do you want me to get you a room for the night?"

"Well, I think I'll wait on that," Brannon replied. "You got a scales to weigh out a little dust?"

"Mama Grande's full of scales," the man said with a wink, "and several of them are almost accurate."

Pulling a small leather poke out of his bedroll, Brannon tossed it to the man. "Well, weigh this on your most honest scales and then tell me how much credit I have coming."

"Yes, sir! I'll do that. I'll treat you fair."

Brannon stepped to the next section of the store, which featured clothing. He considered new trousers and a shirt, but shuddered to think about trying them on before he had a chance to bathe.

The center area was the lobby to the hotel, with rooms located somewhere in the rear. Several men clustered near a table in the lobby, not bothering to look up at Brannon or the other people scooting from one shop to the next.

The cafe was on the far side of the hotel lobby. Brannon stepped softly into the room and glanced quickly at the patrons. Most of those at the tables were men. Most were covered with trail dust. All of them packed pistols.

"Mister, you want to eat?" a woman with white hair and tired eyes called to Brannon. "Or are you just going to stand there?"

"Yeah, ma'am . . . just a minute," Brannon responded.

He lightly stepped into the final "room" in the building, which turned out to be the saloon. It was jammed with men, choked with thick smoke, ringing with the shouts of gamblers. Leaning against the front wall and resting one hand on his pistol grip, Brannon carefully searched the room with his eyes.

No Waldo Vance. And none of his associates.

He stepped back into the cafe, which was separated from the rowdy bar by blankets hanging from a cross timber in the ceiling. Brannon sat down at a small table that backed up against the "wall" to the bar. He could keep an eye on the front of the cafe and the rear as well.

The waitress returned.

"You ready for supper?" she growled.

"Is there a menu?"

"Menu? Look at you. You been in the hills since spring and you want a menu? Are you hungry or not?"

"Yep. What have you got tonight?"

"You can have steak, potatoes, eggs, and bread for a dollar, or stew and bread for four bits, but the stew ain't worth eatin'. I ought to know, I made it."

"I'll take the steak."

"You're a smart man."

"You do have a dollar, don't ya?" she pressed. Brannon remembered his shabby appearance.

"I'm starting a bill. Now you don't suppose you have a smile, do you?" Brannon teased.

"Smile? I don't get paid to smile!" She huffed out of the room.

She had only been gone a moment when Henry marched over to Brannon's table.

"Son, I figure you got—"

"$128 worth?"

"Well, I'll be . . . you had her measured all the time."

Suddenly, Brannon noticed most of the light to his table was blocked. He glanced over to see a woman, almost as wide as she was tall, strolling toward him. Her round face still showed a sparkle that gave Brannon the impression she had once been an attractive woman.

"Are you the *vaquero* wanting a tab?" She let the words fall gently from her mouth.

"And you are Mama Grande?" Brannon nodded, tipping his hat.

She looked him up and down, then shrugged. "Well, you can run up to ten dollars; then I'll need the cash. You looking for a job?"

"Nope."

"Well, what are you looking for? No one comes to Conchita unless they have to."

"I'm looking to buy a change of clothes, a decent horse, a clean room, and a hot bath."

"Well, you won't get that for ten dollars."

"He left a purty good poke with me, Mama Grande," Henry interceded.

"How much?"

"$128."

"$128 in dust?"

"Yep."

Suddenly onto her face burst a smile that seemed to light up the whole dreary, musty room.

"We can get you fixed up. 'Course, can't sell you a horse until morning. A bath, you say? No baths at this time of the year, but, well . . . Henry, get a couple boys to drag that tub out of my room and put it in number four. Yes, sir, I'll even provide a bathtub. Now don't ever say Mama Grande doesn't treat a man right."

"Listen," Brannon asked, "I'm looking for a little man by the name of Vance, Waldo—"

Big Mama pulled a '57 Smith and Wesson tip-up revolver out of her dress sleeve and jammed the .22 caliber barrel against Brannon's temple.

"Do you work for Vance, cowboy?" she hissed.

Brannon had no doubts she would pull the trigger if provoked. "I have never worked for Vance. On several occasions he has tried to kill me, and I was considering returning the compliment."

"Well . . . well . . . well," she said with a sigh, not relaxing the pistol in the slightest.

"I never lie to a lovely lady with a loaded gun," he assured her.

"They can talk purty when you hold a gun to their heads," she said to Henry. "Well, if I catch that Waldo Vance, I'll pinch his head right off that scrawny little body of his. Came in here yesterday and pistol-whipped Henry and stole over two hundred dollars! Ain't nobody in Colorado that can get away with that! Are you really gunning for him?"

"I'd like to see him hang, but I'll use a gun if needs be. When did he leave?"

"About this time yesterday."

"Headin' north?"

"To Denver, I reckon. There was three of them in here. Could have been more outside. One of my boys shot a horse out from under Vance, and he doubled up. I don't suppose they're travelin' all that quick."

"You got a good night horse for sale?"

"You going to leave now?"

"Yep."

"How about that bath and gear you wanted to buy?"

"It can wait. Have you got a horse?"

"Oh, yeah. I've got a big black horse that can outrun the Central Pacific. But it'll cost you fifty bucks."

"Fifty?"

"And that's a bargain," she insisted.

"It's a deal." Brannon rose to his feet and shook hands with the ring-laden hand of Mama Grande.

"I'll get the rest of your poke," Henry offered.

"I'll grab my gear, and you hustle down to the corrals and get that black saddled," Brannon commanded.

"How about the poke?" Mama Grande pressed.

"Save it until I come back," he called.

"And if you don't come back?"

"Split it between Henry and Smiley here as a tip." He nodded to the waitress who was carrying in his steak.

"You get Vance, and I'll give you that horse," she yelled out to him as he sprinted toward the mercantile end of the building.

TEN

By the time Brannon reached the corral, Henry and the Mexican boy had the tall black horse nearly saddled. He stroked the horse's neck as they finished jerking the cinch.

"¿*Como se llama este caballo?*" he asked.

"*El Viento!*" the boy shouted.

"The wind? He does look fast," Brannon commented as he readjusted the saddle and then swung up onto the horse.

He was hurriedly tying his gear to the back of the cantle and placing the Winchester across his lap when he realized that the boy had been telling him something.

"What did he say?"

Henry handed him the reins. "He said that El Viento only has two gaits—walk and fly. Don't try to get him to do anything else."

"Tell the boy that if no one claims that roan in the next two weeks, he can have him!" Then Brannon gently spurred the horse towards the open road north. He could tell by the way the horse pranced that it was ready to run. Once out on the trail and away from the corrals, he spurred the horse again. El Viento bolted like a race horse in full gallop.

The burst of speed shoved Brannon to the back of the saddle. Instinctively, he made a wild grab for the horn with his left hand, regaining his seat. At the same moment, his old black hat caught the wind and started slipping off his head. He reacted by reaching up quickly with his right hand, slamming the barrel of the rifle into his forehead and pinning the hat brim across his eyes.

He jerked up on the reins with his left hand, and El Viento shut it right down, almost causing Brannon to fly out of the saddle and over the horse's head. He caught his breath, took off his hat, and saw that it was now ripped in front. Rubbing his forehead, he found blood starting to trickle down to his eyebrows. He rolled up his hat and tied it to the saddle strings, then pulled out his bandana, which had served to bandage his left hand only a few hours before, and tied it around his forehead and behind his ears. Then, holding the horn and the rifle with his right hand and the reins with his left, he spurred El Viento. Once again they flew off down the northern trail.

The horse's gallop was as smooth and even as any horse Brannon had ever ridden. Even though it was nearly dark, he knew the horse was traveling very fast.

Man, this horse loves to run! Most men live their whole lives without ever riding such a mount.

Through the night they rode with moonlight and horse instinct to guide them. From time to time Brannon slowed the horse down to a walk. And on three different occasions, he dismounted and allowed El Viento to get a drink of water. He led the horse for about a mile after each drink, but when he remounted, El Viento pranced in anticipation.

At this rate we could catch them by morning.

He had planned to take Vance into Denver to stand trial, but now he considered Mama Grande's threat to pinch off Waldo's head.

It might be worth it just to see the look on Waldo Vance's face when she picks him up by the neck.

Brannon had no plan for capturing Vance. He figured there would be at least two others with him—maybe more.

By the time morning started to break, Brannon was cold and sore. With the beaded leather shirt dirty and smelling of smoke and the dried blood on his forehead under the bandana, he figured he could easily be mistaken for a Sioux or Cheyenne.

At a rise in the road north he could see for miles ahead. Leading the horse a good ways off the road, he dropped the reins over the horn and let El Viento graze on the dried grass of the prairie. The road ran straight north, and he strained to see any activity on the trail up ahead. Several miles away, where some leafless cottonwoods crossed the road, he thought he could make out a column of smoke.

Brannon assumed it could be Vance and his party. Taking no chances, he flanked the road, riding high up on the eastern slope of the mountains where he was always higher than the campsite but still in the early morning shadows.

As he drew up even with the camp, Brannon could see three men and three horses hobbled nearby. Without more daylight, he couldn't identify any of the men.

Three horses? I thought they only had two. But they could steal another one, no doubt. Vance wouldn't want to double up very long.

Brannon considered riding on further north and finding a place to stop them on the road, but he wasn't completely sure they would head north. He wasn't even sure it was Vance. He tied El Viento to a sage and climbed up on a boulder to squat in the shadows. He cupped his hands around his eyes, attempting to cut down the glare of sunrise as he tried to distinguish the men at the cottonwoods.

Brannon had no idea where the shot came from.

Hitting a rock behind his head, it sprayed granite chips onto his neck and hatless head. Without thinking Brannon tumbled off the rock and lay flat on his back between two boulders waiting for another shot or sound. He cocked the Winchester.

He heard shouts from down at the cottonwoods.

"Leddy," one voice screamed, "what you shootin' at?"

Somewhere just off his left shoulder and over the rocks, a voice answered, "A mighty fine horse up here, boys—too nice for an old buck Indian!"

He could tell the man was walking straight towards the horse, and just as he heard El Viento snort and prance, he sat straight up and pointed the Winchester at the horse thief.

"Drop it, Leddy, or you'll never ride any horse again!" Brannon growled.

Glancing back at Brannon with his hands in front of him, the man mumbled, "Ain't no breed going to get the drop on me, no, sir."

He spun to fire, but never squeezed the trigger. Brannon's bullet from the Winchester slammed into Leddy almost lifting him off the ground. The blast, fired at close range, startled El Viento, and he jerked free from the sage and tore up the mountain slope.

Brannon turned back to the cottonwoods. Expecting to see the men charge up the mountain, he fired three quick shots into the trees. To his surprise they responded by mounting their horses and spurring wildly up the road to the north.

Brannon could only watch as they crested the rise in the trail. He turned and glanced down at Leddy.

Well, Leddy, you didn't recognize me, but I recognize you. I gave you a chance to walk away from it all at the Little Stephen Mine, but you insisted on siding up with Vance. Now you know what they thought about you.

Brannon began trailing after El Viento.

The big horse had circled around the top of the first rise in the mountain and started heading back to the south. Brannon knew that if he charged the horse, it would bolt and run for Conchita. There would be no human way to catch El Viento at a gallop.

So Brannon began to walk at the same pace as the big black, lagging behind about a hundred steps. Whenever the horse held up and turned to stare, Brannon would turn and walk away. About the third time he did this, El Viento took several steps toward Brannon, narrowing the gap.

For the next several minutes they continued to play the game. Each time El Viento closed the gap between himself and Brannon. Finally, with the horse only ten feet away, Brannon turned his back completely on El Viento and began to walk north. Walking slowly, he went about ten steps, then halted, and stared to the north, still refusing to look at the horse.

After a moment, El Viento brushed Brannon's arm with his nose. Brannon reached back slowly and clasped the dragging reins. Then turning to the horse, he rubbed it behind the cheekbone and patted its shoulder.

"That's a good boy. Yeah, we had a little excitement, didn't we? Well, are you ready to run?"

He readjusted the saddle, tightened the cinch, and swung up into the saddle. He started to untie his hat, but then left it fastened.

Maybe it's better if they don't recognize me. Vance is the only one who knows me on sight.

Brannon clamped his knees tight against El Viento's flanks and spurred the horse. They flew down the mountain towards the cottonwoods.

Brannon guessed that Vance and the others had fled out of fear of an Indian raid.

That should keep them moving and sticking close to the road. If they glance back, it will be towards the mountains.

He crossed the road near the cottonwoods and allowed El Viento to drink from the nearby creek. Then he rode off to the east of the road a good four hundred yards and turned back north. Although he had no clear trail to follow, the rolling hills and sage offered little opposition to the horse's long stride. Even on the prairie the ground was still wet enough from recent rains to eliminate any dust.

Brannon figured he had ridden about eight to ten miles when he came up a draw and over a hill above a stage stop far down on the road. He could see a stagecoach and some horses in the yard, but the people were indistinguishable. He noticed a slight trail from the east that crossed the Denver road just north of the stage stop. Staying down in an arroyo, he came upon the little trail and rode west toward the crossing.

He drew up at the last rise, pulled the bandana off his head, and replaced it with his hat. Then he pulled his coat out of his bedroll and slipped it on over the beaded leather shirt. After he buttoned it, most of the Indian design was covered.

He slowed El Viento to a walk all the way into the yard. Keeping his hat brim down, he scouted for Waldo Vance. From the noise inside, he knew a debate was raging.

"Mornin'," he said nodding at the man changing teams on the stage.

"Mornin', Mister," came the reply. "You headed south toward Conchita?"

"Well, I'm not sure." Brannon dismounted and walked his horse to the water trough. Taking out his bandana, he wiped some of the dried blood from his forehead.

"Say, that's a mighty fine black you got there. Hey, did you take a blow to the head?"

"Yeah," Brannon admitted, "from the barrel of a Winchester. But I don't want to talk about it."

"I ain't no Paul Pry," the man insisted. "Listen, you might not want to go south. Three men rode in here saying that the Indians attacked them at Cottonwood Crossing and killed their companion."

"What Indians?"

"Cheyenne, I suppose. Maybe Arapaho. Who knows?"

"So what's happening inside?"

"Well, Clyde Barstow, the stage driver, says there ain't any Indians around for a hundred miles, and he's got a route to run. But them fellows is trying to talk the passengers into turning around and going back to Denver. He says they'd be safer if they traveled together."

"That stage carry a strongbox?" Brannon asked.

"Why, of course it does. Say, why you asking that?"

"The men were armed, weren't they?"

"Sure, but everybody packs some iron. Take you, for instance, you ain't had your finger off the trigger of that Winchester since you rode up."

"Yep, you're right about that. Just a bad habit. Is there some grub inside?"

"Oh, sure, but it's pretty crowded in there. It's four bits for breakfast. I can bring you out a plate if you like."

Brannon dug a coin from his pocket and tossed the man a dollar. "Pile 'er high, partner. I could eat a double helping."

"Yes, sir, I'll do that . . . yes, sir."

Brannon sat on a bench backed up against the building and listened to the conversation through the open window.

"Mister," a man Brannon figured to be the driver shouted, "I drive the stage, and we are going south. Anybody that wants off can get off right now, but there will be no refunds! I've run this route three times a week for the last six months and haven't seen one Indian except those sleeping in the plaza at Conchita."

Then came a sound that brought a smile to Brannon's face just as the stage attendant handed him a tin plate piled high with bacon, potatoes, and beans. It was the whiny voice of Waldo Vance.

"No gentleman would allow ladies to ride into the murderous scalping hands of such savages. The cruelties they just inflicted upon poor Leddy . . . I wouldn't dare describe in mixed company."

"If you think the ladies need extra protection, you may ride behind the stage and offer your services, but I'm taking the rig south, and we're leaving in five minutes. I'd suggest you eat up quick!" the stage driver concluded.

Brannon carried his food to the far side of the stage, blocking his view of the stage stop.

He scraped down the last of the potatoes. "Thanks for the breakfast. I sorta missed a meal or two. Say, is there any more room on the stage?"

"Yep. Just two women and a gent. You want to ride?"

"I was thinking of it. I might like to see these wild Indians."

"It ain't no game . . . but you look like you might have taken a shot or two."

Brannon nodded. "On more than one occasion."

"Here comes Barstow, ask him. Clyde, you selling any more seats?"

Barstow looked at Brannon's weather-beaten clothing.

"You ain't going to cause any trouble, are you?"

"No, sir," Brannon replied. "Can I ride to Conchita for a dollar?"

Barstow hesitated. " . . . Oh, well, jump in. It's like a parade already anyway."

Brannon walked back over to the attendant. "Listen, would you wait about half an hour, then turn my pony south, and whomp him good in the rump. He'll run all the way to New Mexico."

"Say," the man pulled up close to Brannon's face and whispered, "you ain't going to rob the stage, is ya?"

"Quite the opposite," he whispered back.

"Are you one of them special detectives working for the stage?"

"I'm sorry, friend, but it would be better if I didn't answer that."

"Don't you worry, son. I can sit on it. I knowed when you rode in on that horse that you weren't no drifter. Yes, sir, I could tell. I'll send your pony down the road, yes, I will."

"'Preciate it," Brannon said with a nod.

He climbed into the coach before the others came out of the stage stop and slunk down where he could glance out but not be readily seen. He spotted Vance and the other two men walk over to their horses and mount up.

Soon the stage door swung open, and a startled woman spotted Brannon.

"Oh, my!" she stammered.

Barstow leaned down from the driver's seat. "We picked up one more passenger, ma'am."

"Oh, yes . . . well, excuse me, I was just surprised." She spoke hurriedly as she climbed into the stage and sat across from Brannon. The other couple entered and sat next to her, leaving Brannon with a whole seat to himself.

"Lots of room over here, folks," he offered.

"Thank you," the man in the tight-collared white shirt said, "but we're quite comfortable."

"Suit yourself. Say, I didn't get much sleep last night. Do you mind if I stretch out?"

"Be our guest," one of the ladies replied.

Brannon stretched his legs across the leather stage seat and leaned against the far wall. He pulled his battered black hat low so he couldn't see them, and they couldn't see him. With his rifle lying between his outstretched legs and the seat back, he looked like a man asleep.

"He's dreadfully dirty," one of the women whispered.

"A prospector, perhaps," the man suggested.

"Or a highwayman," the other woman mused. "Did you see the way he clutched his rifle?"

"Oh, my, but the smell! So . . . smoky. Is he asleep? I do hope he is."

Well, Lisa, you always told me I needed a woman around to make me wash up.

It was another half hour of rumbling and bouncing before anyone spoke again.

"Oh, look, one of those men is riding to the lead. Do you suppose he sees the Indians? Do you have your handgun, Nelson?"

"In the valise, my dear. I'm sure Mr. Barstow can handle the shooting. That's what he's paid for, you know."

"Why . . . he's coming back! I think he wants the stage to stop!"

Brannon loosened his grip on the Winchester and slowly removed his Colt from under his coat, keeping his hand and gun concealed. The stage jerked to a halt, tossing one of the women over to Brannon's side of the coach.

"Oh, excuse me!" she exclaimed, but Brannon didn't move.

"Do you suppose he passed out? He could have been drinking, you know."

"Mister, you'd better have a good reason for stopping this stage!" Barstow yelled. "Is there trouble up ahead?"

"Nope, there's trouble right here! Throw up those hands, driver, or this will be the last stage you ever steer!"

"Oh, my! Nelson, it's a robbery!" one woman gasped.

"Sorry, folks, but it's time to get out," one of Vance's men called from behind the stage.

"Mr. Barstow," the man called Nelson blurted out, "what is the meaning of this?"

"Don't argue with men pointing loaded guns," Barstow cautioned.

"Now there's a wise man," Waldo Vance chimed in.

Peeking under his hat brim, Brannon saw Nelson stand at the door and hesitate. One of Vance's men rode by and grabbed his shirt collar and yanked him to the ground. Seeing that, the two women scurried out of the coach.

"Any more in there?" Vance called.

One of the women muttered, "Well, there's a man who's, you know, I think he might be inebriated and passed out."

"Heff, you drag the drunk out of the stage," Vance commanded.

Brannon could see the man's feet enter the stage and felt a hand grab his jacket and yank it up. Brannon whipped his left hand up, jerking the man by the hair and jamming his face into the barrel of the Colt.

"Mister," Brannon whispered, "don't ever, ever grab a sleeping man by the coat!"

Heff turned white at the sight of the cocked .44. Without releasing the man's hair, Brannon spun him around and pushed him towards the door as a shield.

Both Vance and the other outlaw were near the front of the stage.

"Heff, what took you so . . . " Vance's mouth dropped. In an almost demonic squeal, he yelped, "Brannon!"

"Well, if it isn't the unemployed bank clerk turned stage robber, Waldo Vance," Brannon declared.

"Ladies, pick up Nelson there and get back into the stage," Brannon commanded.

"Don't move a step," Vance shouted twice as loudly as necessary.

"Ladies, if you value your virtue and your belongings, get back in that stage right now!" Brannon barked as he and his captive stepped between the outlaws and the passengers.

Nelson dove into the stage pulling the women in behind him.

The first outlaw had his pistol in his hand resting on his saddle, pointed in the general direction of Barstow, the driver. Vance was pointing his gun towards Brannon, which meant aiming at his own man, Heff.

"Driver," Brannon commanded, "roll this rig out of here and don't look back until you reach Conchita!"

"You move that rig, and it'll be the last thing you ever do," the front outlaw threatened.

"He's got a point." Barstow shrugged. "His hand is on the trigger."

"He raises that gun, he's a dead man!" Brannon ordered, "Get this rolling!"

Barstow slapped the reins, and the stage jolted forward.

The lead outlaw whipped up his gun, but took a bullet into his right shoulder from Brannon's Colt. The impact jolted the gunman off his horse.

The quick move surprised Vance, who was unaccustomed to face-to-face gunfire at close range. Looking back at Brannon, he could see the smoking Colt aimed right for him.

The stage rumbled out of sight with neither Brannon nor Vance paying any attention to it.

"Well, it's a standoff, Brannon." Vance stretched the gun towards Brannon and Heff.

"Not really." Brannon's grip tightened on Heff's hair. "You see, if you pull that trigger, your friend dies. Then I shoot you and you die. Now that's a mighty gruesome sight that I'd rather not witness, but all the same, it doesn't threaten me much."

"Back off, Vance," Heff pleaded.

"Listen to the man," Brannon insisted. "Just toss down that weapon nice and slow. Then we'll all ride to town and let a jury decide which of you killed Marshall Rosser. No need for all of you to hang for that."

"You got the killer in your hands, Brannon," Vance whined.

"I didn't finish off no marshall," Heff insisted. "Now I shot him so that Waldo could escape, but he wasn't dead, no, sir, he wasn't. It was Waldo who shot him five times—five times in the back of the head!" Heff shouted out.

Brannon watched the look in Vance's eyes turn to hatred. He knew instantly that Waldo Vance was going to shoot. Brannon jerked Heff towards some sage by the road, but both men stumbled. Vance shot at them, blasting Heff in the belly.

Staggering to his knees, the fatally wounded outlaw yanked his gun and fired towards Vance at the same time Brannon pulled off a round. Vance was blown out of the saddle by the double impact in the chest, and his horse bolted, causing one boot to jerk clear off his foot.

Heff fell face down on the packed roadway.

Stephen Bly

Brannon, his gun cocked, approached Waldo Vance.

He was choking, and both arms lay helplessly at his side.

"Brannon," he coughed, "you're a fool!"

"I'm alive, Vance."

"Alive? Where's your gold mine? You know where it is. Abner Cheney has it, that's where!"

Vance closed his eyes and gasped for another breath. Even as his chest began to fill up with fluids, he rattled on.

"You're a fool, Brannon! You sided with Cheney. He and gunmen like Trevor will be spending your gold while you die of pneumonia by some lonesome trail."

Again Vance struggled to breathe. "You're a fool, Brannon." He could only whisper now. "Not me, I went for it. I almost had it. Twenty men rode with me! The Vance gang, history will record! And you are the biggest fool, Brannon. You picked the wrong side, Mr. Stuart Brannon! It was Trevor who shot old man Davis in the back!"

"What?" Brannon shouted.

"You're a fool, Brannon. Trevor tried to cut out Cheney by making Davis talk. But the old man stood pat, so he killed him! Davis was as crazy as you, Brannon."

For a moment, Vance lay motionless. Then he opened his eyes again. "You tell them . . . it was the Waldo Vance gang. They robbed the stages, they held up Mama Grande's, they . . . they fought it out at the Little Stephen Mine. You're a fool, Brannon . . . you're a . . . "

Vance didn't close his eyes this time.

And Stuart Brannon didn't bother listening for a heartbeat.

Heff and Vance were dead. The third man had a shoulder wound that would heal if the bleeding stopped and he had some rest. Brannon helped the man to his horse, tied his rope around the man's waist, and then fastened it to his saddle horn.

"If you try to outrun me, I'll pull you to the ground," he warned.

He had just strapped Heff's body to the saddle of the third horse when he heard someone approaching at a gallop from the north. Whipping out his gun, Brannon recognized riderless El Viento bearing down on him.

"Whoa!" he shouted. "El Viento, whoa!" Brannon waved his hat at the horse, who never lost a step or swerved an inch. Thundering past Brannon, the horse crested the hill and continued towards Conchita.

Brannon stood there shaking his head.

Then he strapped Vance's body on top of Heff's and mounted Waldo Vance's horse.

Leading the horse with the two dead men and following the roped and wounded outlaw, Stuart Brannon rode south to Conchita.

ELEVEN

Mama Grande led the parade of curious onlookers carrying lanterns as Stuart Brannon pushed and pulled his cargo into the village square at Conchita. It was long after sunset, and most of the village was asleep.

She hefted up her long dress and waddled across the windy courtyard to examine the bodies tied to the last horse.

"Well, *vaquero agotado*, you have been a busy man," she commented.

"Yes, ma'am," Brannon replied. He swung down off the saddle and called out to the shopkeeper, "Henry, help me get this old boy down. He's lost a lot of blood and will need some medical attention before he's sent off to trial."

The shopkeeper scurried over to help as the others inspected the dead. "El Viento came in this afternoon," he commented. "But he didn't say nothin' about how the shootin' turned out."

"That's a great horse," Brannon said smiling, "if you can keep it from going back to Mama Grande. Have you got a doc around here?"

"Yes, yes." Henry called, "Mama Grande!"

"She's the doc?"

"Doctor, judge, lawyer . . . you name it."

"Well, Mama Grande," Brannon called, "can I count on you to take care of this man?"

"Oh, it will be a pleasure to attend the man who robbed me and used my Henry's head for a drum!" she said with a leer.

The wounded man shot a terrified look at Brannon.

"Well, Mister, a man reaps what he sows. It happens to be the best I can do for you now."

Mama Grande ruffled her way up to Brannon. "You brought that pinheaded Vance to justice. El Viento is yours. There isn't anybody in Colorado ever accused Mama Grande of backin' out of a deal."

"Thank you, ma'am, but I'm willing to buy him from you."

"You would insult me by refusing my offer?"

Brannon bowed his head. "I would not insult such a lovely woman as yourself for any reason. I accept your offer."

Mama Grande cackled out a deep laugh. "*El vaquero agotado* doesn't see well in the dark!"

"Listen, ma'am, can you still shove that bathtub down to a clean room?"

"*Vaquero*, tonight, just for you, Mama Grande would move mountains." She rolled back across the street to the hotel.

"She moves mountains every time she takes a step," Henry whispered.

The Mexican boy wandered out to the plaza and took charge of the horses.

"Henry," Brannon called, "did the stage pass through here today?"

"Yep. Say, Barstow said you left your Winchester in the stage, so I tucked it behind the counter over at the store. Old Barstow said you pulled a fast one on those highwaymen. He figured you might be a Wells Fargo agent. Are you working for the stage line?"

"Nope." Brannon let the subject die. "You got the mercantile still open?"

"Oh, no, she's closed down . . . well, say, of course, if you need anything, I'd be proud to open it up for you."

"'Preciate it," Brannon said nodding. "What I'd like to have is some fresh clothes, a bath, clean sheets, and three days' sleep."

Stuart Brannon sorted through the dry goods in the dim lantern light of the mercantile. He grabbed a pair of brown duckings, a heavy gray wool pullover shirt, and a new pair of suspenders. The tall stovepipe boots in the case happened to be his size. And he sorted through a dozen beaver felt hats before he found one that fit.

"You got a water kettle boiling on that stove in the back room?" Brannon asked.

"Yep, sure do."

"Well, let me steam this brim to shape, and I'll buy it."

On his way to the back room Brannon grabbed up several other items including some socks and a new red bandana. "Listen, Henry," he shouted from the back room, "grab me your best winter coat. Something heavy and stout. Don't give me something that'll rip the first time I get bucked off a horse."

Brannon pulled the sweat-stained hatband off his old hat and fastened it on his new one. He tossed the old one into the corner, placed the new one on his head, and returned to where Henry was figuring up the bill.

"Add in two boxes of cartridges," he concluded.

"Well, sir, including the bullets, it comes to . . . well, it comes to $31.14. Now those boots were twenty dollars. If you'd like—"

"I'll take 'em, Henry. I've still got a poke full of credit around here, right?"

"Yes, sir, you do."

"Do you happen to know which room I'm bunkin' in?"

"It's number four."

"Thanks, Henry . . . and listen, could you pop over there to the cafe and see if anyone's still around. I'd sure like to have that steak and potatoes now."

"Mr. Brannon, I'll bring it to your room."

"Listen, Henry, you cut yourself a two-dollar tip from that poke. Nobody should work extra without extra pay."

"Why, yes, sir, thank ya!"

Brannon was surprised to find that the tub had already been moved to his room, and it had two feet of steaming water in it.

As he pulled off his boots and trousers, he examined the small adobe-walled room. The wood plank floor was smooth from wear, but clean. The mattress had real cotton stuffing, not straw.

Bright curtains hung at the shuttered window. Each bed leg stood in a coffee can full of water, assuring the sleeper a bugless night. A dresser, pitcher and bowl, and a clothes rack completed the furniture. There was even a faded flyer on the wall that advertised bullfights in Monterey.

But best of all, there was, jammed near the door, a beautiful galvanized iron bathtub. With soap and rag in hand, Brannon slipped into the water. He wasn't at all sure where the dirt left off and the skin began. He wasn't in any hurry to find out.

When he finished scrubbing his hair, Brannon sank low into the tub and flopped the hot dripping washrag over his face. It was one of those moments he wished could go on forever.

It didn't.

There was a hard rap at the door.

"Come in, Henry!" he shouted without lifting the rag off his face. "Just sit that steak—"

The door opened, then slammed shut.

Brannon splashed his way to a sitting position and glanced around the room for his pistol.

Again there was a knock at the door.

"I said, come in, Henry!"

A feminine voice startled him. "I am not Henry, and I have no intention of coming into your room!"

Brannon instinctively grabbed his towel and wrapped it around his midsection even though he was still under water.

"Yes, ma'am, I'm sorry. I didn't think I'd have visitors this time of the evenin'."

"Well, I'm Miss Harriet Reed. I was on the stage with you this morning."

"Yes, ma'am, I guess we weren't introduced. I'm Stuart Brannon."

"Yes, I know that now," she replied. "I just wanted to stop by and apologize for our awful behavior on the stage. We . . . eh, we said some things that should never have been said. I'm afraid we treated you rather shamefully."

"Yes, you did, Miss Reed." Even though the door was closed,

Brannon still clutched the water-logged towel around his midsection.

Harriet Reed continued, "Please forgive us, Mr. Brannon. As you could tell, we are new to the West, and there are many things we don't understand."

"Apologies accepted. If you will still be here, may I buy you and your companions breakfast in the morning?"

"Only if you will let us pay," she insisted. "We would feel much better about that."

"I might be a little late in the morning. I haven't slept in two days—and haven't been in a real bed in months."

"A late breakfast will be fine. Ah . . . Mr. Brannon, may I ask you a rather personal question?"

"Eh . . . as long as you don't embarrass me."

"Mr. Brannon, how did you get a room with a bathtub? We were told there were no bathtubs available."

"Well, I think I might of smelled so bad that Mama Grande felt sorry for the other guests in the hotel," he said laughing.

"Yes, I believe you might be right," she added. "We will see you for breakfast."

Finally pulling himself out of the tub, Brannon dried off and pulled on a brand new pair of white long johns. He had just pulled back the comforter on the bed when there was a knock at the door.

"Just a minute," he yelled. "Don't open that door!"

Hopping on one foot and then on the other, he yanked on his new pair of duckings. He cracked the door just a few inches. Henry stood there with a plate of hot food.

"Say, you ain't got a woman in there, do ya?" the old man asked.

"Good grief, no!" barked Brannon. "Come in, come in."

"Well, I just didn't want to come barging in when I wasn't supposed to." He set the food down. "There's two steaks there for the price of one. Some drunk passed out before his was served. The cook didn't want it to waste."

"Henry, what time do you start work?"

"Seven o'clock. Why?"

"Well, come up here about 7:30 and throw me out of bed."

"What?"

"I'll need to get around in the morning, and I can tell you it will be a major battle. Come in my room and pound on my head if you have to."

"Sure thing, Mr. Brannon." Henry turned and started to leave.

"Say, eh . . . you don't sleep with your hand on the pistol, do ya?"

"Not usually." Brannon grinned.

"Just checkin'." Henry shuffled on out of the room.

Stuart Brannon knew that there were greater thrills in life than going to sleep in a clean bed at Mama Grande's in Conchita.

But at that moment, he couldn't think of any.

Some dreams just mimic the present.

Others remind a man of his past.

Occasionally, they predict the future.

All Brannon knew for sure was that this dream was not of the present. All night long he had been riding the smoothest cutting horse in the world—plunging into the herd of bawling cows and calves, pushing to the outside, first left, then right, then left, then straight on. Then the flankers on the ground took over, and Brannon spun back into the herd for another.

No maguey tied hard and fast.

No lariat to dally.

Not a hoolihan thrown.

Cuttin' in, cuttin' out.

All night long.

It was a pleasant dream.

The clothes were stiff, but Brannon reveled in their cleanness.

"Maybe I should have bought a tie," he mumbled to himself as he pulled on new boots and slung the bandana around his neck.

There was a swift knock at the door. "Mr. Brannon, it's me, Henry. Time to roll out!" Poking his head in the door, Henry waved. "I see you don't need no help this mornin'."

"How are you feeling, Henry?" Brannon asked.

The store clerk smiled. "Fine, thanks. Say, them folks from the stage is waiting for you in the lobby."

When he reached the little room that served as a lobby, only Mama Grande greeted him.

"Ai, yi, yi!" she smiled. "*Vaquero intrepido* has arrived!"

"Well, I figure a fella ought to pull on new clothes once a year." He grinned.

"I believe your friends seated themselves in the cafe," she reported. "Will you be leaving today?"

"Yes, ma'am."

"I surmised that. I'll have El Viento saddled and brought around to the front. Take care of him," she urged.

"He's a fine horse."

"And take care of yourself," she added.

The cafe was only half full when Brannon entered. It was easy to spot Harriet Reed and the other couple. They looked out of place.

The man stood to greet him. "I'm Nelson Barton, and this is my wife, Gwendolyn. I believe you've met my sister-in-law, Miss Harriet Reed?"

"My heavens, Mr. Brannon," Miss Reed exclaimed, "I would hardly have recognized you!"

Nelson sat back down. "Since there's only one breakfast on the menu, we ordered for you," he commented.

"'Preciate it, folks. And sorry for the excitement yesterday. I figured that Vance and the other two were going to hold up the stage, and I just couldn't think of any other way to stop it at the time."

"Mr. Brannon, are you a lawman?" Mrs. Barton asked.

"No, Mrs. Barton, I'm not a lawman, but I certainly believe in obeying the laws."

The light conversation continued as they were served their food. Brannon hesitated, then looked at the others.

"Folks . . . eh, I don't want you to take offense, but, well, I haven't had time to sit down and enjoy a meal in a cafe with people like yourselves in quite a long time. And . . . it's a little habit of mine to give the Lord thanks."

"That would be very nice," Miss Reed said and bowed her head.

After a short grace, conversation picked up again quickly.

"Mr. Brannon," Nelson Barton quizzed, "tell us, what kind of work do you do? I mean, if that's not an intrusion."

"I'm a rancher turned prospector."

"How exciting!" Miss Reed said smiling. "Surely your wife doesn't travel with you?"

Brannon finished chewing a big bite of potatoes. "My Lisa died almost two years ago now."

"Oh, I'm sorry," Miss Reed stammered.

"I wandered up here alone looking for a friend of mine. I didn't find him, but I found a little gold. So now we're going to dig it out, and then I'm heading back to Arizona to buy cattle."

"Arizona?" Miss Reed asked.

"Yes, ma'am."

"Anywhere near Prescott?" she queried.

"You'll do a little better if you pronounce that Press-cut, rather than Pres-cot," he corrected. "But, no, my ranch is not very close to Prescott. It's over on the eastern side of the state. Do you have an interest in Prescott?"

"Yes," Barton informed him, "I'm the new federal land agent in Prescott. So the ladies are moving with me."

"Well, we just might see each other again," Brannon said with a nod. "When I get back, I'll be wanting some acres to add to my place, I'm sure."

"How delightful!" Miss Reed exclaimed. "You will have to stop by for tea."

"Harriet," Mrs. Barton complained, "we can't invite guests when we don't even have a home to call our own yet."

Brannon started to reply, but a voice from the front of the cafe caught his attention.

"I suggest that table by the gentlemen and ladies," came a familiar British accent.

"Fletcher!" Brannon called.

"Brannon! My word, is that you? In Conchita? But, the . . . the mine . . . and plans, and . . . " he stammered.

Fletcher and Velvet Wendell came over to the table. Brannon jumped to his feet and began the introductions.

"Eh, Mr. and Mrs. Barton and Miss Reed, these are my business partners, Edwin Fletcher and Miss Velvet Wendell."

"Miss Wendell?" Harriet Reed questioned. "Then you and Mr. Fletcher aren't married?"

"Not hardly," Velvet Wendell stated. "A girl couldn't marry Edwin without getting Queen Victoria's permission first. And your name was Mrs. . . . "

"*Miss*—Harriet Reed."

With one quick flick of the eyes, both women inspected each other.

Brannon took charge. "Folks, it's been really good to have breakfast with you. But as you can imagine, my partners and I need to discuss a little mining business, so if you'll excuse me."

"I'll look forward to seeing you in Prescott, Mr. Brannon," Harriet Reed said pleasantly.

"Yes, ma'am." Brannon bowed, and then turned to his partners.

"Edwin, you and Vel will just have to postpone breakfast for a while. We need to settle a few matters." Brannon hustled the two out the door of the cafe, down the wooden sidewalk, and across the courtyard to the short adobe wall around the plaza.

"Brannon, what's going on here?" Fletcher quizzed.

It took a good thirty minutes for Brannon to fill them in on the marshall's death and the fate of Vance and his men.

"Trevor shot Everett Davis!" Fletcher choked.

"Well, Waldo Vance made that quite clear, and dying men don't lie much."

"How can you prove it?" Velvet asked.

"I tried to figure that one out all day yesterday. Guess we could accuse him and see if he cracks," Brannon suggested.

"Will that work?" Fletcher asked.

"If we are convincing enough. We could let it be known that we have someone to testify against him."

"Who?" Wendell asked.

"You." Brannon smiled.

"Me? But Everett Davis told me he had no idea who the man was."

"Trevor doesn't know that."

"I say, Brannon, would all of this jeopardize Velvet's safety?"

"Yep."

"Then I simply must protest!"

"Fletcher, a lady doesn't need two big brothers!" Velvet insisted. "I would like to apprehend Mr. Davis's killer as much as you two."

"Then we'll need to . . . wait a minute!" Brannon stopped himself. "You didn't tell me what you're doing here. You're supposed to be in Denver by now!"

"Well, when we reached Tres Casas, there were no wagons to be purchased. So we just took the ore samples to the assay office there."

"In Tres Casas? They have an assay office?"

"Oh, yes, Tres Casas has changed a lot," Fletcher informed him. "Well, the ore is high grade, and they opened a line of credit for $10,000 at the bank."

"Bank?"

"Yes, but we still needed to round up the big boys in Denver to finance the excavation, so we bought a few things and have been on the trail for several days," Wendell concluded.

"Brannon, I still can't believe you left the Little Stephen. I would have sworn that a thousand violent savages couldn't have budged you," Fletcher stated.

"They couldn't. Velvet's words about Everett settling accounts before he passed on hit me hard. I had a few accounts unsettled."

"Really, Brannon, leaving the mine to the Utes? How do we know it will still be ours when we return?"

"We don't. Maybe you two don't understand. I can survive whether I have that gold mine or not. But I realized that I couldn't live with myself for letting Everett's death and the marshall's go unrectified. Look, that's just the way I am."

"Well, partner, where should we head now?"

"The Little Stephen."

"All three of us?" Fletcher protested.

"Yep. We'll have to reclaim the mine, and we'll have to face down Trevor."

"Now surely Velvet—" Fletcher again began.

"Fletcher," she protested, "I can make my own decisions, and I can take care of myself."

"Well, I really don't think you realize the danger this would—"

Suddenly, Velvet spun on Fletcher and slammed her right elbow into his stomach. He doubled up, and as he did, she locked her fists together and crashed a windmill uppercut to his chin. He sprawled over the adobe wall into the little plaza.

"What in heaven's name was that for?"

"Well, Edwin, you may be right. Maybe only two of us should return to the mine!" Brannon laughed. "By the way, Miss Wendell, that green and black dress looks lovely on you."

"Thank you, sir, and I might add that a bath does wonders for your appearance as well."

"And new clothes—you did notice the new clothes!" he urged.

"Of course, but they're rather conservative, maybe even a bit dull. However, I suppose they could impress ladies in Prescott!"

Rather dull, Stuart Brannon? Lisa, you're up there laughing, aren't you?

"Brannon, I say, Brannon," Fletcher broke in, "would you look at that horse!"

"Seventeen hands, black, and he won't stand still at the rail," Brannon mused without turning to look.

"Whose horse is he?" Wendell asked.

"Mine."

"You bought that horse!" Fletcher exclaimed.

"Nope. He's a gift."

"A gift?" Velvet Wendell raised her eyebrows. "Surely not from Miss Reed and friends?"

"Nope. From Mama Grande."

"Mama who?" She squinted as she spoke.

"Mama Grande. She owns the whole town."

"Well," she sniped, "she must have a very large heart."

"Everything about Mama Grande is very large," Brannon quipped.

The trio purchased several other needed items, a pack horse, and presents for Red Shirt and his friends. By noon they felt prepared to recross the mountains and return to the mine. The plan was to settle in at the Little Stephen. Then Brannon and Wendell would go down to Tres Casas and confront Trevor.

Less than an hour on the trail, before they reached the turnoff to the pass, they met Deputy Giles heading back to Denver. He was stunned to learn of the marshall's death. Brannon finished describing the tragedy to the deputy by drawing a map in the dirt to show where he had buried Marshall Rosser. He unfastened his new bedroll and handed the deputy the marshall's hat and badge.

"You say I can pick up the only remaining gang member at Conchita?"

"Yeah, providing Mama Grande hasn't used him for a pin cushion. I've got a feeling that old boy will tell the whole story just to save his neck. I tried to bring in Vance alive, but he went wild. Nothing I could do."

"Can I get a wagon up to the grave?" the deputy asked.

"There's no road, but you can wind your way up through the sage. You going to take his body home?"

"He'd do it for me," the deputy said with a sigh.

"You going to need any help?" Brannon asked.

"Not on this side of the mountains. I'll go into Conchita and rent a wagon. A couple of Mama's boys can ride out with me. You heading back to the mine?"

"Yep, if the passes haven't snowed over," Brannon answered.

"Well, if I were you, I'd stay out of Tres Casas for a while," Deputy Giles cautioned.

"Did Mr. Cheney pull through?" Velvet Wendell asked.

"He's healin' up fine, ma'am. But he fired Trevor, who went on a drunken shooting rampage just south of Tres Casas. I stuck around a few days to help Sheriff DuPrey track him down and toss him in jail."

"Tres Casas has a jail?" Brannon asked.

"Anyway," the deputy continued, "when I finally left, Trevor was sitting in there threatening to kill Cheney, the sheriff, me, and Brannon."

"Nice guy," Brannon said with a nod.

"Well, good luck, and good-bye, ma'am." Giles tipped his hat at Velvet.

The three of them rode up the slope straight into the afternoon sun. They stopped at the first crest of a hill and looked back at Conchita in the distance.

"We're going into Tres Casas no matter what the threat, aren't we?" Wendell asked.

"Yep."

Brannon pulled his new hat low and spurred El Viento into a gallop.

TWELVE

It only takes three long, tough days to cross the mountains and make it to the upper reaches of Trabajacito Creek.

Provided it's summer . . . and it doesn't rain . . . and you don't run into Utes . . . and your horse doesn't fall off a ledge.

Late October is not summer.

For Stuart Brannon, Edwin Fletcher, and Velvet Wendell it was a long, tough seven-day ordeal. By the first evening, it had started to snow. When they got above timber, the snow whipped straight into their faces. Heavy winter clothing suddenly felt paper thin.

Somewhere just past the crest, the trip to the Little Stephen Mine changed from one of expediency to one of survival.

Every numb finger, every aching lung, every freezing night in the snow by a dying campfire reminded Brannon of the previous winter.

Lord, here I am again! The whole scene is repeating itself! I haven't accomplished anything! It's snowin' and I'm freezin'. Not another winter up here!

Descending the mountain proved to be more treacherous than the climb up. The rain-wrecked trail was now covered with several inches of snow that melted off during the day and froze solid at night. On day four, Fletcher's horse lost its footing and tumbled down an embankment. Both the horse and Fletcher came out of the spill with a limp. He walked his horse most of the rest of the way.

On the fifth day, the pack horse with most of the supplies

slipped off the mountain into a jagged canyon, making recovery of the horse or gear impossible. Only El Viento seemed impervious to the danger of slipping. The big black gelding pranced on the ice, always looking as if he were searching for a wide green meadow in which to run. Brannon and Fletcher saw little more of Velvet than her bandana-covered face peering out of Everett Davis's buffalo robe.

By day six, the storm had broken, and the sun became the sole occupant of the deep blue sky. On that day the ice refused to melt at all, and they knew that cold weather had arrived to stay. Brannon figured the trail east through the mountains would now be closed until the following summer.

The glare of the sun off fresh snow gave a different view of La Plata Canyon. Gone were the light greens of cottonwoods and aspens. Twisted trunks and spindly limbs presented a bleak appearance. Even the spruce, pine, and fir now had such a thick blanket of snow that little color showed.

As they broke camp on day seven, all three were beginning to doubt the wisdom of anyone spending the winter at the mine site.

"Look, Brannon," Fletcher offered, "this is the way I see it. We closed the east pass, correct?"

"Yep," Brannon said with a nod.

"Well, couldn't we just secure the mine . . . you know, mark it off, seal the entrance, and come down out of the canyon together. We'll probably just make it through Brighton Pass before it closes."

"I don't have any feeling left in my face," Velvet Wendell complained. "I mean, I can see my hand come up and touch my cheek, but I don't feel anything at all!"

"I'll tell you one thing, no gold mine on earth is worth anyone else losing their life," stated Brannon. "If we can't put up something winter-proof, we'll all go down together. We've fought for months to establish that claim. We'll just have to make sure we open up the trail in the spring. If we go down and sit on Cheney all winter, who is going to try to jump claim?"

"What bothers me," Fletcher mused, "is that the sheriff is waiting for you in Tres Casas."

"What bothers me," Brannon said pointing his Winchester up over the next ridge, "is all that smoke!"

Wendell and Fletcher gazed up into the bright sunlight to notice several thin columns of winding smoke drifting up over the crest of the western mountain.

"Is that the Trabajacito?" Wendell asked.

"It sure isn't Prescott, Arizona," Brannon mumbled.

"Well, I see Stuart has his mind on Prescott again," she teased.

"Red Shirt should only have one fire going. There's got to be a dozen fires over there."

"Which means?" Fletcher quizzed.

"That old Cheney got well a lot quicker than we imagined and brought up a cavalry regiment to guard the mine. Or Trevor is out of jail and found more drifters to camp out with him."

"Or," Fletcher added, "perhaps Red Shirt has accidentally set the forest on fire."

"One thing is certain," Brannon said grimly, "we've got to sneak up on camp and survey the situation. We won't be taking the trail down. It will be watched or guarded."

At the crest of La Plata ridge, Brannon led the others off the trail and into the trees. From that elevation, it was difficult to distinguish objects at the mine site. The glare of bright sunlight off the new snow almost kept them from seeing anything at all. They dismounted and walked to the edge of the trees.

"What do you see?" Wendell asked as she shuffled her way out to Brannon, still dragging her buffalo robe.

Stuart Brannon had his hat pushed back on his head, and his gloved hands circled his eyes, trying to provide a better view. Fletcher climbed up a nearby boulder and also attempted to trace the smoke columns back to their origin.

"I say, Brannon, how many friends does this Red Shirt have?" Fletcher glanced down at Brannon.

Still staring at the canyon below, Brannon mumbled, "Eh . . . two—Crazy Waters and Chalco. What do you see?"

"Maybe you better come up here," Fletcher called.

"The Army? Did Cheney actually send in the troops?"

"Well," Fletcher said reaching to pull Brannon up, "I don't think it's the U.S. Army, but it does have the looks of an army."

Brannon stared down the canyon for several moments.

"I don't believe it!" he gasped.

"Is that what I think it is?" Fletcher probed.

"What is it? What do you see? Edwin, give me your arm. Help me up," Wendell insisted.

"How many do you count?" Brannon asked.

"Well, that's the problem; they blend in with the snow."

"What blends in with the snow?" she called, trying to catch her breath.

"I think I can count fifteen," Fletcher answered.

"Yeah, well, I figure maybe up to twenty or twenty-five." Brannon looked at Fletcher and Wendell.

"Twenty-five? There are twenty-five men down there?" Wendell asked. "You mean Vance's whole gang returned?"

"Oh, no, it's not Vance's men," Brannon informed her.

"Whose then?"

"Red Shirt's, I presume," Fletcher said sighing.

"Oh, they're Utes, all right," Brannon agreed.

"My word, there are twenty Indians down at our mine?"

"Even that wouldn't be too bad," Brannon replied. "There are twenty teepees! That means there are probably one hundred to one hundred and fifty people down there!"

"One hundred and fifty!" Violet Wendell cried. "We can't fight all of them!"

"Nope." Brannon jumped off the rock into the foot-deep snow around it. "It looks like Red Shirt invited his relatives to a party."

"Do you suppose they will all move on now that we have returned?" Velvet asked.

"I don't know. It depends on whether Red Shirt is still alive, whether he told the truth to the others, and whether any will be happy that our 'presents' are strapped to the broken back of a pack horse at the bottom of a canyon."

"All right, General Brannon, what's our tactic? And please don't tell us to charge straight at them!" Fletcher helped Velvet Wendell off the boulder.

Brannon shook his head. "Not this cowhand. We got to go down through the trees, try to single out Red Shirt, and have a little conference. Whatever you do, don't start shooting unless your life is in immediate danger."

"But you never had any trouble with the Utes, right?" Wendell asked.

"Look, dealing with three likeable warriors is one thing, but dealing with a whole tribe is a different matter."

Brannon kept them back in the trees all the way down the mountainside. They had to ride far south of the mine to avoid the clearing and then come back up to the edge of the trees.

"Isn't it too cold for them to winter here?" Fletcher whispered.

"We'll soon find out." Brannon pointed to the teepees as several warriors mounted up and rode straight at them. "They've seen us. Don't shoot, and don't look nervous."

"He's joking, right?" Velvet gulped.

"Nothing scares Brannon," Fletcher murmured, "nothing but pretty women and God. Not necessarily in that order."

"It's Red Shirt!" Brannon said softly but never took his eyes off the Indian on the paint horse nor his finger off the trigger of his Winchester. He spurred his horse into the clearing to meet Red Shirt head on. Fletcher and Wendell trailed behind keeping between Brannon and the creek. The two parties, all on horseback, stopped about ten feet from each other.

"The Brannon has a nice horse," Red Shirt said without expression.

Glancing at a brand-new black hat with two eagle feathers in the band, Brannon commented, "And Red Shirt has a nice hat."

Suddenly Red Shirt broke into a dimpled smile. "Reward from Chief Ouray himself!"

"The Big Chief? You went to see the Big Chief?"

"No, Chief Ouray came to Red Shirt. This is his camp!"

"He's here?"

"The center teepee is his."

Brannon scanned the teepees in the clearing and those pitched along the creek. "Where are the women and children?" he asked.

Red Shirt looked straight at Brannon, but he didn't speak for several moments. "It is hunting camp," he finally replied.

"And just what are you hunting?"

Red Shirt broke into a cheek-to-cheek grin, but did not speak.

"Well, we have returned so you may go on with your hunt now," Brannon suggested.

"The Brannon is a lucky man," Red Shirt informed him.

"Oh?"

"Yes, Chief Ouray say that the Brannon and friends are free to travel across Ute land on his way south to the desert. He promised that he would not attack you."

"Well, we are quite fortunate," Brannon agreed. "However, this is our land, remember? And you can tell Chief Ouray that the Brannon said he is free to travel our land until he returns to his home."

"The Brannon is not showing great wisdom," Red Shirt insisted. "This is not your mountain. This belongs to the Utes."

"No! Everyone knows that Ute land begins at the Little Dolores."

"Everyone is wrong. Chief Ouray is very wise. Red Shirt knows very little. Chief Ouray says no white men may come north of the hot springs."

"The hot springs? Brannon, we found our gold on Indian land?" Fletcher probed.

"It's their word against ours," Velvet Wendell called.

"No." Brannon silenced the others. "There's about a one-hun-dred-and-fifty-to-three chance that they're right."

"You mean, we just walk away from it all?" Fletcher asked.

"Well, we could try running away, but walking sounds safer."

"We're giving up our mine?" Velvet asked incredulously.

"At the moment, we don't have any options." Brannon kept his eyes on Red Shirt. "Did you enjoy the food?"

Red Shirt motioned with his hands as he talked. "Yes, but it is gone."

"Don't look for any more from me. Red Shirt does not keep his promise."

The Indian cocked his rifle, but when he lifted it up, he looked straight into Brannon's raised Winchester. Neither man lowered his gun.

"Red Shirt does not break promises. We kept all white men away from your hole in the ground. It is white men who lie. They promised that none of the gold men would dig on Ute land."

"Where are our belongings?"

"In a pile by the creek. Chief Ouray is a generous man. He says you may take what belongs to you—including the hole."

"How are we going to pack out that gear?" Fletcher called.

"We aren't, and he knows it," Brannon answered with a shrug. "Tell the great Chief Ouray that those things are presents to him from the Brannon."

"He will be happy. I think he will not kill you."

"That would be nice."

"I told him it would take two men to kill the Englishman and three men to kill the woman—"

"Really, now," Fletcher mumbled, "I say!"

"And I told him it would take twelve good men to kill the Brannon."

"Was he willing to pay that price?" Brannon asked.

"Yes. He has thirty men along the trail south. You will not make it to the falls unless Chief Ouray so decides."

"Tell Chief Ouray that we are riding out right now. If, in the days to come, it is proved that the mine is on Ute land, we will not return. But if it is shown that this land belongs to us, one hundred teepees could not keep me away!"

"I will ask him to call off the warriors on the trail." Red Shirt turned his horse back to camp. "I will tell him."

Brannon immediately led his little troop towards the creek and the trail down the mountain.

"We're leaving? That's the end of it?" Velvet Wendell demanded.

"I don't want them to change their minds. That's not a hunting camp. It's a war camp. We're lucky to have a hair left on our heads."

Two gunshots sounded from the middle of the camp.

"Are they shooting at us?" Fletcher asked pulling his pistol.

"A signal to clear the trail, I hope." Brannon looked back to see Red Shirt ride to the creek, alone this time.

"The trail is clear," he called. Then he paused and added, "The Brannon will always be welcome at the humble fire of Red Shirt."

"And Red Shirt will always be welcome at the humble fire of the Brannon, but you may not bring your whole family next time!"

Red Shirt broke into a dimpled grin, spun his paint back toward the teepees, and raced away.

Without another word, Brannon led Fletcher and Wendell down the trail. They hardly spoke all the way to the frozen falls of the Trabajacito.

"Do you think we've ridden out of their sight?" Wendell asked.

"Maybe," Brannon replied.

"Where to now," Fletcher probed, "Broken Arrow Crossing?"

"We'll camp at the hot springs," Brannon suggested. "If it's clear tomorrow, we'll ride over to the Crossing."

"And if it's storming?" Velvet Wendell pressed.

"Then we're going straight for Brighton Pass before it closes in. That gold mine was the only thing that could convince me to winter out up here again."

After several more miles on the trail, Fletcher spoke up. "Brannon, are we really riding away from all that gold?"

"We'll check with an Indian agent. But until they build a fort on the upper end of the Trabajacito, we can't do anything about it. Indian land is Indian land."

"Surely a man like Cheney knew that," Fletcher commented.

"I don't think so. I don't think any of us considered this Indian land."

"But we have papers on it," Wendell reminded him. "What about the papers?"

"Worthless, if this is Indian land."

"We just give up?" she pressed.

"No one could hold that mine now without federal troops stationed up here, and if this is Indian land, the troops won't be sent. Vel . . . there are some times when it's best just to give up."

"Maybe for you two. Do you know what kind of life I get to

go back to?" she cried. "Scrubbing tobacco juice off some splintered floor, washing dishes for room and board, doing laundry for some dirty, smelly miner, trying to keep the drunks from carrying me upstairs!"

"Look, Vel, I'm sorry it didn't work out. It was going to be my ticket back to the ranch. It was worth the struggle. And we gave it a good fight. It wasn't completely wasted. After all, you got to spend most of the last month with two fine gentlemen," he said laughing.

Velvet Wendell rode in silence for several moments.

"You're right, Stuart. I gave it a good try, didn't I?"

"Yep. Now let's go give Trevor a try," he said with a nod.

"Brannon, you almost sound happy to get rid of the mine," Fletcher called.

"Well, it simplifies life a bit," Brannon said softly. Then he broke out laughing. "False claims!"

"What's he mumbling?" Fletcher asked.

"False claims, Fletcher. Don't you see the humor?" Brannon shouted.

"What?"

"Look at it this way. We spent months fighting off all those who would jump our claim, only to find out that we had a false claim to the place to begin with!" Brannon was nearly hysterical with laughter.

"It's not exactly my type of humor," Velvet Wendell observed wryly.

"Don't complain." Fletcher shook his head. "I haven't seen him this happy since the spring thaw!"

THIRTEEN

Brannon, Fletcher, and Wendell descended Brighton Pass on the front edge of the first big snowstorm of winter. As they got lower, the snow turned to rain, and then thinned out to dark scattered clouds by the time they entered the outskirts of town. It was nearly two weeks since they had left Conchita.

"Does Tres Casas have a hotel?" Velvet asked.

"It's grown a bit, Vel," Brannon answered, "but I would guess that Nadine Montgomery's is still the best place to stay. Tell her you're a friend of Everett Davis, and I'd imagine you'll get royal treatment. Check and see if she has three rooms."

"Where are you going?" she asked.

"Well, Sheriff DuPrey threatened to arrest me if I came to town, so I'll go visit him first."

"You want to be arrested?"

"Nope, but I don't want it hanging over my head either."

Fletcher rode up by Brannon. "Stuart, did it ever occur to you that some of these men on the sidewalk might have been the ones with Vance up at the mine?"

"Yeah, I thought about that, but most of them never saw our faces, right?" Brannon turned to Wendell. "Vel, I hope you don't think I'm just acting like big brother again, but I think maybe Fletcher should go with . . . I mean, if it seems like a good thing to you . . . you know, it's—"

"Edwin," she said sighing, "Stuart certainly gets rambling and incoherent every time he's in a crowd. I believe it would be terribly boring for you to get stuck riding down the street with him. Perhaps you'd like to join me in riding over to Nadine Montgomery's?"

"Thank you for offering me an escape." Fletcher tipped his hat.

Brannon turned El Viento up Main Street and stopped the first man who crossed in front of him.

"Partner, I'm lookin' for Sheriff DuPrey. Could you point me to his office?" he asked.

"Down there on the left . . . right past the church." The man pointed south.

Church? Tres Casas has a church? Lord, what have You been up to?

Recent rains had left the the streets of Tres Casas puddled and slippery. Brannon worked the big black horse around the water, paying little attention to the busy activity in the shops on main street. Two quick shots came from the direction of the sheriff's office. Brannon spurred El Viento to the hitching post at the wooden sidewalk.

Bystanders gathered around outside the office as Brannon reached the door with his Colt drawn in his right hand. He banged on the door. "Sheriff DuPrey? Sheriff, are you in there?" Turning to one of the bystanders, he motioned. "What happened in there?"

"Who knows?" One man waved his hands above his head. "I ain't going in there!"

"I told Sheriff DuPrey not to lock Trevor up. That man's mean."

"Trevor's still in there?" Brannon asked.

"He was."

"Is there a back door?"

"Sure, in the alley."

Brannon dashed behind the building to find that door swinging open in the breeze. With hammer cocked, he entered the office and found Sheriff DuPrey sprawled on the floor, shot twice in the chest.

"You men out in the street," he yelled, "get a doctor over here!

The sheriff's been shot!" Brannon knelt down by the lawman. "DuPrey, this is Brannon. Did Trevor do this?"

"A sneak gun," DuPrey coughed. "He had one of those sneak guns. Tried to get me to unfasten the cuffs."

"Did he get the key to the cuffs?"

"Nope," DuPrey gasped. "Brannon . . . get him for me. You're the only man I know who could face him down. I tried. I tried hard."

"Sheriff, the doc's on his way . . . where's the blacksmith in Tres Casas?"

"Behind the livery." Sheriff DuPrey clutched his heaving chest.

Two men from the street burst through the front door. Brannon left the sheriff with them and raced out the back and down the alley toward the livery. He circled behind the blacksmith's shop and strained to listen through the back door. He heard iron bang against iron at the anvil, and he heard a scared man.

"I'm hurryin', Mister . . . that gun makes me nervous. This is hardened steel . . . it ain't pot metal, you know!"

Brannon quietly lifted the latch on the door and started to swing it open. Suddenly, the whole back door fell off its hinges and crashed into the blacksmith's shop just as Trevor's shackles broke.

Brannon dove behind a couple of kegs of horseshoe nails as Trevor grabbed the blacksmith around the neck and shoved his gun at the shaking man.

"I don't know who you are, Mister, but if you want this blacksmith to live, you'll toss that gun out and get over here where I can see you."

"Thanks, Trevor, but I can see you just fine from right here."

"Brannon? Brannon, is that you?"

"I'm glad you remembered."

"Brannon, I'll shoot him; you know I will."

"Yep, that's your style, Trevor. Unarmed men you can shoot in the back." Brannon rolled quickly behind some sacks just as Trevor fired off two shots in his direction.

"Mister," the blacksmith cried, "don't let him shoot me. Please, Mister, I've got a wife and kids!"

"Trevor, you wasted two bullets. That's not wise," Brannon called out as he sneaked behind a stall.

"Get out here, Brannon, or this man's dead!" He cocked the pistol and laid the hot barrel against the man's temple.

"He's going to kill me, Mister. He's really going to kill me!"

"Trevor, I'll make you a deal!"

"I don't need a deal."

By now, Brannon could see a crowd form outside the front door of the blacksmith's.

"Listen, Trevor, if you don't get out of here soon, you'll never make it."

"That crowd won't stop me!"

"I don't know. They seemed to like the sheriff. I figure they'll have you hung before supper."

"What kind of deal?" Trevor called.

Brannon tossed a horseshoe against the far wall, prompting Trevor to squeeze off another round.

"Now you're just down to three, Trevor. Well, here's the deal. You toss down the sheriff's pistol . . . and your sneak gun. Then turn the man loose and let him out the front."

"And you shoot me?"

"Nope."

"Let them hang me, right?"

"Nope."

"What's the deal, Brannon? I'm in a hurry!" he screamed.

"You grab that horse in that stall behind you and lead it over here to the back door. You mount up and ride out the alley."

"You're going to let me ride away? I'm no fool, Brannon!"

"And I'm no liar," Brannon added. "You once made Vance back off because you said it wasn't right to shoot an unconscious man. Well, I don't forget things like that. But my standards are just a little different. I don't shoot men who are unarmed."

"You aren't going to let me just ride out of town, Brannon."

"I didn't say you'd make it out of town, but I promised I wouldn't shoot you. Now a minute ago you didn't seem to think anyone else in town would stand up to you."

"That's a fool's game, Brannon!"

"Look, if you shoot that man, then I shoot you, and you're dead. If you let him go, you might get a break and outrun the posse."

"I don't have a chance without a gun. No deal, Brannon."

"Wait!" Brannon called. "You keep the gun, but shove it in your holster until you clear this building. Don't hurt the blacksmith. Come on, Trevor, the crowd's getting bigger!"

"Brannon . . . " Trevor stopped in midsentence. Shoving the blacksmith towards the front door, he dove for the horse's reins. "Either I'm a fool, or you are, Brannon! But I'm not going out that back door! I'm going out the front door. That way Mr. Stuart Brannon will have to shoot me in the back. And me with my gun holstered."

"I won't shoot you, Trevor!"

"If you try it, I'll kill the first three people in that crowd . . . you know I will!"

"I believe you, Trevor. I said I wouldn't shoot you."

"You're a fool, Brannon."

"Like Everett Davis was a fool?"

"That old man was the biggest fool of all. Stubborn as granite. It took two shots and a few kicks in the back before he would even hint at where your claim was. Kept sayin', 'Brannon will settle this score! Brannon will settle it!' I should have let Vance shoot you!"

Stuart Brannon knew exactly what he was going to do next. It wasn't an easy decision. Even the thought of it rubbed him wrong.

Lord, I don't like this. You know I don't like this! What else can I do? God, help me.

Trevor, gun holstered, mounted up and walked the horse towards the open double door at the front of the blacksmith's shop. His back was toward Brannon, and his hand rested on the pistol grip.

Brannon raised his Colt and aimed directly behind the right ear, steadying the pistol with his left hand.

If I do this right, he'll be dead when he hits the ground!

Trevor had just cleared the door when the shot rang out, and the whole crowd out front dove for cover, expecting more bullets to fly.

Stuart Brannon sprinted to the doorway in time to kick the half-drawn pistol out of Trevor's hand and jammed his own gun in the back of Trevor's head.

"You shot my horse!" Trevor screamed. "I can't believe it—you shot my horse!"

"I kept my promise," Brannon declared. Then he called to the crowd, "You men, help me pull him out!"

Several men came forward, including an out-of-breath Edwin Fletcher.

"My word, Brannon, we can't leave you alone for ten minutes!" he puffed. "Did you really shoot the horse?"

"*Semel insanivimus omnes.*" Brannon shrugged.

"Well said," Fletcher mused.

"A couple of you men go find the deputy," Brannon ordered.

"We ain't, ain't g-g-got no deputy," the blacksmith stuttered.

"Well, then, you be the deputy! Somebody's got to watch him."

"No, sir, no, sir, I ain't going to guard Trevor!"

Others in the crowd backed away.

"You got a mayor?"

"Sure!"

"Well, get the mayor and have him meet me at the jail."

With Trevor disarmed and hands tied behind his back, Fletcher and Brannon walked him down a crowded street towards the jail.

"Brannon, listen, this isn't the best time to do business, but you'll never guess who I ran into over at Nadine Montgomery's."

"Mama Grande?"

"No. Abner Cheney is there! Naturally, I told him about the mine, and now listen to this, he actually offered to buy us out."

"What?" Brannon blurted out. "You did tell him about the Utes?"

"Certainly, but he said that someday the U.S. government would move them off that land, and he could wait."

"So why pay us?"

"He doesn't want any prior claims on the whole mountain. I don't know—it sounds strange, doesn't it?"

"Unless he knows what the government plans are already." Brannon pondered. "What did you tell him?"

"Why, that the partners would have to talk it over, of course."

"Where's Vel?"

"She and Mrs. Montgomery hit it right off, so I suppose she's found a bath and some clean clothes."

Brannon marched a sullen and silent Trevor off to the small jail cell at the sheriff's office. After snapping one padlock on the cell and another on the back door, Brannon and Fletcher stepped out to the street where a crowd of people had gathered.

"Are you that marshall from Santa Fe?" one man asked.

"Nope," Brannon replied.

"You, eh . . . ain't on the run, are ya?"

"Just a concerned citizen," Brannon said with a nod. Then he turned to Fletcher. "You think Cheney's offer was sincere?"

"A bit bizarre, but sincere. He's a happy man, Stuart. I don't think he's got anything to gain by deception," Fletcher responded.

"Happy? Cheney is happy? What'd he do? Foreclose on all of Tres Casas?"

"I don't have any idea. Maybe he's just happy to be living," Fletcher offered.

"Say," Brannon asked one of the bystanders, "we sent for the mayor, but he hasn't showed. Could you track him down for us?"

"He's busy," one man reported.

"Busy?" Brannon barked.

"Yeah, he took the sheriff over to the doctor's office."

"Well, he can let the doc look at Sheriff DuPrey. I need to see—"

"The doc is the mayor!" the man replied.

"What?"

"Yep, Doc Shepherd is the mayor. Best one we ever had too, though some folks say he's too young," an older man commented.

"Listen, we'll baby-sit Trevor until the mayor comes. How about one of you trotting over to Nadine Montgomery's and bringing us a plate of supper? We've been on the trail awhile."

"That's obvious," one woman with an umbrella mumbled.

"We ought to hang that Trevor," one man shouted.

"Yeah, he don't deserve to live!" another hollered.

"Well, men, out of respect for Sheriff DuPrey I think you ought to wait to see how he pulls through. That way you'll know just what old Trevor does deserve."

The street was windy and cold. In a few minutes Brannon and Fletcher reentered the office and lit a lantern.

"Well, Trevor, the lynchers are screaming for you," Brannon reported to the prisoner.

Just as Brannon flopped back into the sheriff's chair, the office door swung open with a clean and well-dressed Velvet Wendell carrying two plates of food.

"Well, Miss Velvet," Fletcher said smiling, "you do look lovely."

"Thank you, Mr. Fletcher." She set the meals on the desk and glanced in at Trevor. "Mr. Brannon, you seem to bring out a shooting everywhere you go."

"You noticed that too?" Fletcher chimed in.

"Well, this time it happened before I got here."

"Nadine said Trevor shot the sheriff, and you chased him down."

"Nadine? You and Widow Montgomery got chummy real quick. Did you land a job with her? Everett used to say she was quite a lady."

Velvet Wendell glanced at Fletcher and then at Brannon. "Did you tell Stuart what Cheney said?"

"About buying our useless claim?"

"He doesn't think it's totally useless," she insisted.

"If it's a serious offer," Brannon added, "he must be light-headed from that wound."

"He's light-headed, but not from the wound," she retorted. "Anyway, I told him I was sure you would accept the offer."

"You told him what?" Brannon groaned.

"Sounds good to me," Fletcher commented.

"Look, Stuart, it's a great chance for me, and you said we were walking away with nothing anyway," she argued.

"What do you mean, a chance for you?" Brannon asked.

"See, Cheney has asked Nadine Montgomery to marry him."

"What?"

"I say, Cheney getting married?" Fletcher stammered.

"But Nadine said she wouldn't move until she sold her place. So Cheney was there when I told her all about our problems at the mine. He offered $2,500 to each partner of the Little Stephen."

"Why $2,500?" Fletcher pressed.

"Because," Brannon guessed, "Nadine wanted $2,500 for her business, right?"

"That's right!" Velvet affirmed. "And she'll sell it to me as soon as you agree to sell out to Cheney."

"So old Abner Cheney is buying himself a wife," Brannon said grinning.

"Brannon, he loves the lady. You do understand love, don't you?" she chided.

"You're right. A good wife might be the ticket for Abner. It'll keep him home more. He won't be able to high-pressure prospectors so often."

"Then you agree?" she quizzed.

"Edwin?"

"Quite so, old boy. I'm sure the Mulroneys could use some extra funds."

"We won't be able to get into Broken Arrow Crossing and visit them until spring, of course," Brannon added.

"Well," Fletcher said taking a bite of steak, "it wouldn't hurt us a bit if we had to eat food like this all winter. It would certainly beat your beans!"

"You could have cooked any time you—"

"Would you two quit sticking your head in the wheel and give me an answer!" Velvet shouted. "Are we taking Cheney's offer or not?"

Brannon stood to his feet and shouted back, "Yes, Miss Wendell! You're the agent for the company. Now go squeeze it out of the old man in gold!"

Suddenly Stuart Brannon was almost floored by a tearful Velvet Wendell who threw her arms around him and hugged his neck with all her strength. By instinct, he hugged her back. It had been a long, long time since he had felt a woman's touch.

"Heh, er . . . hum," a voice stammered at the door. "Is this a bad time to stop by?"

She released Brannon, and all three turned to see a man standing at the open door.

"I didn't mean . . . I'm Mayor Shepherd, and—"

"Come in, Mayor," Brannon invited. "It was just a little celebration. Mayor Shepherd, I'm Stuart Brannon. This lady is Miss Velvet Wendell. She and I are . . . sort of like brother and sister."

"Oh?" the doctor raised his eyebrows.

"And this is Edwin Fletcher, and he's like another brother," Velvet explained.

"Well, Miss Wendell," the doctor said with a smile, "you have a large family."

"It's a strange one, all right. If you gentlemen will excuse me, I've got a business deal to complete." She turned and raced out the door.

"Mayor," Brannon addressed Dr. Shepherd, "how's Sheriff DuPrey?"

"Not good. I don't know if he'll pull through."

"Did you get a statement from him?"

"He told me everything."

"Well, then, you know you need to appoint someone to fill in for him."

"There's not a lot of qualified men in Tres Casas."

Brannon leaned back in the sheriff's chair and took a bite off a biscuit. "Oh, you'll find someone around town."

"The sheriff did have a recommendation."

"Oh?"

"He said, 'Appoint Brannon.'"

"I say, that's a splendid idea," Fletcher remarked.

"Sorry, I'm not staying in town that long. Besides, did the sheriff also tell you he had threatened to arrest me if I ever came to town?"

"Yes, he did. That's why he mentioned you. He said, 'Brannon's an honest man and too tough to arrest. We either have to shoot him or make him sheriff.'"

"Brannon, what else will you do all winter?" Fletcher quizzed.

"How about sleep?"

"Totally boring."

"Well," Brannon said with a sigh, "I do want to see Trevor get what's coming to him."

"Then you'll take the job?" Mayor Shepherd asked.

Brannon stared at Fletcher, glanced at Trevor behind bars, and finally back at the mayor.

"Two conditions," he offered. "First, it's only temporary. If the sheriff recovers, the job goes back to him. If not, then I only hang on until Brighton Pass opens up in the spring."

"You going up to Rutherford City?" Mayor Shepherd quizzed.

"What?" Brannon and Fletcher groaned.

"I hear they changed the name again," the mayor reported. "A memorial to the Rutherford brothers, I suppose. Although God only knows why anyone would want to remember them."

"I doubt if it was God's idea," Brannon mumbled.

"You said two conditions. What else do you need?" the mayor asked.

"A deputy," Brannon announced.

"Oh, I'm afraid that Tres Casas couldn't afford two lawmen."

"Well, this old boy will work for free, right, Edwin?"

"Surely you jest," Fletcher mumbled.

"That's his way of saying, 'I'd be delighted!'" Brannon said with a laugh.

"Listen, I'll go round up the city council, and we'll meet right here within a half-hour. Can you hold things down until we get back?" Mayor Shepherd queried.

"We'll still be eating supper," Brannon replied.

As soon as the mayor walked out the door, Fletcher exploded. "I say, Brannon, this is irregular. I mean, I'm not even a citizen. You can't expect me to—"

"Oh, hush, Edwin. Think of it in your memoirs. It would make a splendid chapter for Lord Fletcher."

Fletcher paced across the wooden floor.

"I say, Brannon, you have an excellent point! Deputy to the legendary Stuart Brannon!"

"Not hardly a legend." Brannon laughed.

"You haven't read my memoirs." Fletcher smiled. "You don't suppose Nadine Montgomery has a cup of decent tea, do you?"

"I believe the new owner is a Miss Velvet Wendell, formerly of Brannon, Fletcher, Mulroney & Wendell," Brannon offered.

"It's turned out to be a rather exciting day," Fletcher observed.

"Lots of prayers have been answered. Cheney's got a wife. Vel has a business. We got a few dollars out of the mine, and we don't have to winter it out up there."

"And Tres Casas has a new sheriff," Fletcher quipped.

"Temporary sheriff," Brannon corrected him. "Why even Trevor is having his prayers answered."

"Trevor? How do you figure that?"

"Everybody prays if they get scared enough," Brannon replied. "Old Trevor hasn't been lynched yet—must be an answer to his prayers."

"I'll kill you, Brannon!" Trevor screamed from the cell.

"Oh, don't encourage him," Fletcher scolded Trevor. "Haven't you figured it out? Brannon works better under pressure!"

Within the hour, Brannon and Fletcher had been sworn in as the Tres Casas police force. Mayor Shepherd returned to care for Sheriff DuPrey, while two of the city councilmen spelled off the new lawmen guarding Trevor.

After breaking up a brawl among the "ladies" at the Ugly Duck Saloon and taking guns away from two drunks, Brannon and Fletcher walked into Nadine Montgomery's.

Velvet Wendell greeted them in the hall.

"Vel, Fletcher and I will be your first customers. We're going to need those rooms until spring, it looks like," Brannon ordered.

"The Davis & Wendell Hotel is proud to have such prominent citizens," she said grinning.

"Davis & Wendell . . . I like that name," Fletcher commented.

"So do I," she said.

"Edwin, you take the 10:00 P.M. shift at the jail. I told them we'd be back by then. I'll come over at 2:00. We'll have to spell each other off until Trevor stands trial. Velvet, you don't want me on clean sheets without a bath. Where's the tub?"

"In the little room at the end of the hall." She pointed.

"Send some hot water down while I take El Viento to the livery." Brannon turned and clomped out of the room, spurs jingling.

"Well, Edwin, there goes a happy man." Velvet sighed.

"I don't believe Brannon ever lived an uneventful day in his life," Fletcher added.

"Would the deputy like to join me for tea, or does duty call you also?" she asked.

"Tea? I say, a Fletcher would never refuse tea. Besides, with Sheriff Brannon loose on the streets, another lawman would be superfluous, don't you agree?"

In her best English accent, Velvet curtseyed as she said, "Quite, correct, Lord Fletcher, quite correct!"

Stuart Brannon walked slowly back from the livery, stopping by the front of the bank and checking the door. His mind raced to plan a schedule for him and Fletcher.

We need the mayor and councilmen to keep helping as long as Trevor is behind bars. Then if we staggered our shifts, most of the hours would be covered.

Stopping in the middle of the muddy street, he glanced up at the dark night just as the clouds parted enough for a bright star to shine through.

Well, Lord, it's not exactly a thousand head of cattle, but it does seem more worthwhile than digging in a frozen mountain all winter.

Thanks.

Brannon took one more look at the quiet Tres Casas night and then pushed open the front door of the Davis & Wendell Hotel.